I0566471

# Temptation in the Pulpit

### Black Romance Author - Church Drama

# By: Eddie Johnson

## Rare Jewels Publishing Company

# Also by Eddie Johnson

*Reaching For Celestial Heights*

*The author prohibits any reproduction of this book without his authorization. Brief excerpts are permitted for reviews and articles. Any real life individual resemblances are purely coincidental. Situational dialogue and character interactions are products of the author's imagination.*

*www.EddieJohnson.net*

*www.RareJewelsPublishing.com*

*Copyright © 2014 Eddie Johnson*

*ISBN: 978-0-9827188-3-4*

*Text use: Bible verses from the King James Version of the Bible (Public Domain)*

## Chapter 1

Georgette Bradbury glided down an isle of True Life Divinity Baptist Church. Minister Devon Tucker's eyes were fixated on her as he watched her every stride. The petite, six foot, auburn complexioned beauty took a seat on a pew directly in front of the pulpit. Georgette had delivered on her promise to Minister Tucker that she would attend Sunday morning service. She was a recent Jersey City Seminary graduate.

Following the benediction, members quickly dispersed and headed for the exits except for a few, which hung around to socialize.

"Sister Bradbury, I would love to have a word with you," Devon uttered.

Georgette made a sharp turn with the heels of her stilettos in the thick plush carpeting losing her balance. The good minister reached out and helped her to regain her footing. "Thank you, Minister Tucker. How are you?"

"I'm fine. We are glad you are here. Maybe one day you can start gracing these halls on a permanent basis."

"I flew into town last night. I look forward to meeting with your Assistant Minister Advisory Selection Committee. I will be here for a week. My half sister Marjorie will be putting me up at her house."

"Tell Marge, I said hi. Your resume is quite impeccable. I hope you make a good impression during your interview."

"I'm honored by your kind words," Georgette gracefully responded.

"I hate to break off our little chat; but I have to run off to an impromptu meeting called by the Deacon Board."

"Take care, Minister Tucker."

"Please Georgette, call me, Devon. I think we should get to know each other on a first name basis."

"Okay, Devon. Hopefully, we'll get to know each other on a more professional level."

"If it's the Lord will," Devon murmured.

Georgette carefully turned and walked out the front entrance.

Realizing he still had a few minutes to spare, Devon went to his office to check his emails. His

Personal Assistant Amelia James walked in with a cup of coffee.

"Thank you, Ms. James."

"You're welcome, sir. Just a reminder, you have a meeting in ten minutes. Also, Ms. Bassett the head of the Women's Ministry dropped by earlier and left a packet for you." She laid it on his desk and proceeded to leave.

He pulled the information out of its holder. "They're considering setting up a Caribbean cruise," he mumbled.

Ms. James stopped in her tracks, turned around, and then asked, "Were you trying to get my attention, pastor?"

"I'm sorry, Sister James, I was thinking aloud. I was saying the Women Ministry would like me to bless their effort to set up a church cruise. They have my blessing. I would never stand in the way of good Christian fellowship. I think it's a great idea."

"Sign my fiancé and I up, we're ready to set sail. It could be our pre marital excursion."

"I hear you sister."

Ms. James continued on her way.

After taking a sip of the fresh brew, Devon briefly checked his cell phone, and read a text message from Kimberly Su Chung. Today marked their tenth month dating anniversary. Kim as she preferred to be called is of African American and Chinese descent. Her message simply said that she missed him and could hardly wait to accompany him to dinner. The dinner at a four star hotel would denote the official kickoff of The True Life Divinity Baptist Conference. True Life Divinity was a mega church in South West Orlando. The annual conference had become well known within the United States and abroad. Once he finished perusing his emails, he rushed off to meet with the Deacon Board.

During the meeting, it was brought up that a Mr. Jeffrey Bradbury had donated to the church building fund. Deacon Seth Roberts proceeded to add fuel to the conversation. "Rumor has it that he sold his majority ownership in an automobile dealership in Chicago and that he's relocating to Orlando."

"I wonder if he's related to Georgette Bradbury. She is one of five remaining candidates vying for our vacant Assistant Pastor position," Devon said.

"Jeffrey Bradbury is her husband," Deacon Johnson asserted after he chuckled and cleared his throat.

Devon tapped his pen on the table. "That explains her wanting to minister at True Life Divinity. He will probably make a good tither, if he decides to join our congregation. Deacon Watkins, I know you can attest to the fact a generous donor could finally allow us to break ground on our new envisioned place of worship."

"I agree, pastor. Hopefully, the advisory committee will make a decision that will most likely benefit the church," Deacon Watkins the church treasurer asserted.

"I'm sure the committee is aware of any information that we are privy to and more," Deacon Board Chairman Brandon Roberts provided a word of caution. "We don't have to put forth any undue influence. There is no need to stir up controversy among the members. Rumors are very easy to start and can be very hard to stop."

## Chapter 2

The majority of True Life Divinity's congregation was out in force to their annual conference dinner. Devon and Kim had arrived ahead of time so the minister would have adequate time to rehearse his message. Exiting off Interstate Highway 4 the downtown Orlando skyline lights provided a magical view. Devon maneuvered his Mercedes to the front of the hotel. The valet promptly took possession of the vehicle. The couple entered the grand lobby of the hotel where they were welcomed by staff and directed to its banquet hall.

"Hi Minister Tucker," Marjorie called out.

Devon and Kim suddenly stopped and noticed her approaching them from an adjacent entrance. "We're glad that you made it to tonight's festivity," Devon stated.

"I'm Marjorie Stevens. Georgette Bradbury is my half sister."

"I met Georgette earlier today. She mentioned that you are providing her lodging. "Marjorie, I would like to introduce you to my lovely lady Kim Su Chung."

"Hi Kim, I think the good minister has his hands full. You probably have broken a few hearts in your day."

Kim turned her head and focused her attention on Devon.

"Marjorie's half sister has applied to be the next Assistant Pastor of True Life Divinity," Devon promptly interjected.

"That's great. I wish her luck. Now getting back to your remark Ms. Marjorie, I'll be true to my man as long as he is true to me!" Kim snapped.

"Kim, I was merely complimenting your good looks. You misinterpreted my statement. I wasn't trying to berate you." She peered across the room at her table. "Looks like my guest have arrived. You guys, enjoy your night."

Devon took notice that Georgette was one of her guest. As Devon and Kim walked over to their table, he observed Kim looking a little down. "Are you okay?"

"I'm fine," Kim replied.

"There is no reason for your loyalty to be called into question. Sister Marjorie was wrong. However, it's a good example of the type of situations that first ladies often encounter."

"Should I take that as an unofficial marriage proposal," Kim wittingly quizzed Devon.

"I was merely talking about Sister Marjorie's unholy demeanor."

Devon pulled out a chair for Kim. Once seated they were greeted by their guest.

The church dignitaries at the table were namely Deacon Board Chairman Roberts, Treasurer Watkins, respective spouses, and his Personal Assistant Ms. James.

Ms. James teasingly referred to Kim as True Life Divinity's next first lady. Others at the table complimented her choice of evening attire.

The headwaiter started making his rounds of the tables. He took time to welcome everyone prior to presenting the evening cuisine. Their waiter would soon follow, taking their orders, and returning promptly with their meal request.

Throughout dinner, a local gospel choir, and orchestra provided a soul stirring evening of entertainment. Afterwards, Minister Tucker took to the stage. He delivered a rousing sermon that had some of the sister's in attendance caught up in the spirit. He preached about avoiding sinful temptations and remaining true to the Lord. This sermon rang especially true for Devon. A couple of years ago it was rumored that he was quite a ladies' man. A particular young woman in the congregation had been named and accused of having an affair with their fearless leader. The Deacon Board demanded his ouster. A recall election was held in which the church voted overwhelmingly to retain their embattled minister, failing to believe the unproven allegation. Some of his esteemed parishioners believed that he was back to his old cheating self after finally getting over the bitter divorce with his ex wife Karen. The couple divorced amongst his purported infidelity. Devon's new leading lady Kim chalked up the recent rhetoric as baseless accusations from a pool of desperate women trying to compete with her for the single minister's hand.

The next day, Georgette met with the Advisory Committee. She candidly answered their questions as they drilled her to no end.

During the interview, Georgette was asked by Chairman Darlene Ricks to explain briefly her qualifications. She mentioned being the daughter of a Baptist minister and while growing up having participated in almost every ministry within his church.

Georgette noted how she diligently served as the youth pastor at her father Carlton Hatcher's church Heaven's Shore Baptist for over two years, until she recently relinquished the position due to an impending move to Orlando.

Deacon Johnson's wife Trina presented Georgette with an unexpected question. "Georgette, I would like to know if you are harboring any secrets that could potentially surface later, which could cause shame to this great church."

Georgette knew she would have to lie if she expected to prevail in her quest. "I don't have any secrets that I can think of which would fall into that category. I have always lived an upright life."

Georgette also fielded questions about her time spent at college. In doing so, she was not remiss in reminding them that she graduated in the top tier of her class.

Chairman Ricks also imparted a tad bit of information about her seminary training in Jersey.

Finally, Georgette was given time to talk about the love of her life, Jeffrey. After she complimented him as being the ideal husband, the interview ended.

# Temptation in the Pulpit

The Chairman informed her that they would be in touch.

As soon as Georgette left the meeting, she immediately called her husband. He was relaxing at home. "How did it go?" Jeffrey asked. "Were you able to knock them off their feet?"

"I did my best. I should know in a few days if I'm going to make the final cut."

"Jeffrey, hold on a moment I have another call." After putting him on hold briefly, she returned. "I'm going to have to call you back; mom is on my other line."

Having hung up with Jeffrey, she reiterated the information to her mom.

"I wish you well babe. I don't see any reason you should not be a finalist," Susan said.

"I'm sure the other contenders are equally confidant in their ability to succeed if given the chance and they're probably not withholding secrets from the committee. I would like to grow in the Lord's Ministry, however, I wonder if I am worthy."

"Hold up your head. Do not allow the devil to kill your blessing. The abortion took place before you met your husband. You were right by not sharing that information; it should stay buried in your past."

"I take full responsibility for my actions."

"Sometimes I wish you would not be so hard on yourself. You truly love Jeffrey and I'm sure that he loves you."

"Mom, I don't want to talk about my marriage. I was saying how I feel unworthy of the position before we somehow got off track."

"That's what I though we were discussing."

"Minister Thomas Miles was weak. He found me irresistible. Common sense should have prevailed; but he did not think twice about the potential consequences of our unholy sexual act. I'm at fault too; I could have stopped him when I realized his intent. If word of my aborting a fetus gets out this could signal the end of him being pastor at Blessed Truth in Jersey City; and to me being an assistant minister in Orlando, should I get the position."

"Nevertheless, your father and I believe you deserve to be chosen." Susan tried to show support for her daughter and to put her mind at ease. "If the Lord is on your side, perhaps you don't have anything to worry about."

## Temptation in the Pulpit

"Okay mom, I'll try to be strong for my parents."

## Chapter 3

Jeffrey flew into Orlando International airport on a chartered private jet were he was met by Georgette who had been patiently waiting. Disembarking the plane Jeffrey could not help but notice the wide smile on his wife's face as he walked down to the base of the air stairs greeting her with a warm embrace and kiss. Leaving the airport the couple stopped at a restaurant on Semoran Boulevard for an early evening meal. Jeffrey delighted in talking about his stake in two upstart businesses in the local area. He envisioned being the owner of a deep sea fishing operation and being a minority partner in a venture that would run a riverboat cruise on the Intracoastal Waterway along the East Coast of Florida. The twelve-hour cruise would stop periodically at marinas boasting nearby shopping and dining.

Setting out from the restaurant, Jeffrey would travel the Beach Line Expressway to Interstate Highway 95 into Daytona Beach where they would crossover the Intercoastal Waterway to the world's most famous beach to kick back at an ocean front condominium.

Restless in bed, later that night, Georgette prayed she would not give into advances from Devon. Somehow, she seemed tempted by Devon's mere presence. Lord, you know, I am attracted to Devon. The man is fine; however, I do not wish to entice him into lusting after me. I have been down that road before with Minister Thomas Miles. I just want to do thou will and minister to your flock. Help me to remain faithful to my husband and not fall sway to the man's sinful advances. O Lord, if it's thou will, I would love your blessing to become Divinity's Assistant Pastor and to one day head my own congregation. Amen.

Jeffrey and Georgette had their eyes set on a dream home in the prestigious Bangor's Island Community of Central Florida. The following morning, after a thorough walk through of their future residence, paperwork was finalized to take possession of the property.

Georgette received word from the Assistant Minister Advisory Selection Committee toward the end of the second week of their getaway, which stated that she was one of two candidates still in contention for the position. Georgette would have to schedule and deliver a sermon before True Life Divinity's parishioners within the next two months. She would spend countless hours trying to settle on the right bible scriptures to base her special message.

## Chapter 4

Georgette's True Life Divinity preaching debut found her speaking to a Sunday morning full house. Her husband, mom, and stepsister were on hand to show support. Georgette lifted her head from veering at her text as her father walked through the doors. His flight had been delayed. The lady preacher proceeded to deliver the word. Her message resonated especially well with women, centering on Jesus and Mary Magdalene. Georgette felt an electrifying energy coursing throughout the sanctuary as if the place had been set on fire by the Holy Spirit.

After Church, Jeffrey drove Georgette over to a nearby deli. Carlton, Susan and Marjorie met them at the restaurant."

"You didn't really think I would miss my daughter's preaching audition," Carlton said staring Georgette in the eyes.

"Well, you came awfully close to missing my message," Georgette playfully pouted.

"I never anticipated the layover at Atlanta's Hartsfield-Jackson Airport," Carlton explained the reason for his last minute arrival.

"I thank the Lord you made it in the nick of time, otherwise, we may not have forgiven you," Marjorie noted.

"I am also grateful," Susan spoke and then partook of a morsel of food from the tip of her fork. "When traveling you should always allow for the unexpected."

Georgette tried to solicit help from Jeffrey in trying to convince her parents, once they retire to consider a move to Orlando.

"That would be ideal; however, your parents may be content living out their final days in Chicago. Am I right, Mr. Hatcher?"

Jeffrey's question to Carlton appeared to have had fallen on deaf ears.

Susan glanced at her husband before turning her attention to Georgette. "Your father doesn't have an answer for Jeffrey since we never discussed moving to Florida."

Departing the restaurant, everyone went straight to Marjorie's house, except Georgette, and Jeffrey who checked into a nearby luxury hotel.

Georgette's cell phone belted out a gospel ringtone. Jeffrey picked it up from the nearby dresser. Devon asked to speak with Georgette. He turned and noticed Georgette entering the bedroom. She had been in the kitchen putting on a pot of coffee."

"Who is it?" She asked.

He held the receiver away from his face. "Pastor Devon from Divinity would like to speak with you." Jeffrey returned to the call. "Hold on a moment. She'll be right with you."

He noticed Georgette's face suddenly lit up as she placed the phone to her ear.

"Hi Devon, I wasn't expecting to hear from you."

"Hi, I'm calling to commend you on a job well done."

Your sermon was superb and the way you engaged the congregation, you had them eating right out of your hands."

"Really Devon, you sound as if I have already won them over."

"I heard Zach Jenkins last Sunday."

"And how was he received?"

"He failed to make the same kind of connection."

"Thanks for your vote of confidence. Your kind words are really appreciated."

"If I was completing a score card, you would be leading him in every category."

"I hope you're right. I always make an extra effort to prepare my sermons and then I pray to the Lord to direct me in the deliverance."

After Georgette finished the call, she noticed a disparaging look on her husband's face. She walked over to Jeffrey. "By the look on your face, you have something to say."

"Yes. It's actually a question. It has to do with Devon."

"I'm confused by your remark. "Georgette sensed what sounded like a tinge of jealousy in his voice. "You sound perplexed."

"I want to know the reason Minister Devon would call you prior to the church vote," Jeffrey demanded. "Why would he do that? He should be impartial to whoever is selected."

Georgette reached out and held his hands. "You're right honey. I don't know what motivated him to call. However, I'm not going to lose any sleep over it and neither should you."

# Temptation in the Pulpit

## Chapter 5

Before heading back to Chicago, Jeffrey accepted
an invitation to go fishing with Dexter Jones a potential business partner. Their fishing outing took
them to Jupiter inlet in South Florida. Dexter
backed up his burly pickup truck with his 18-foot
boat in tow to the water. Minutes later, he stirred
the boat away from the shore while striking up a
conversation. "A few months ago you stated that
Velma Dixon your ex personal assistant from Chicago would be relocating to Orlando."

"Well that is still her plan," Jeffrey said. "Velma
recently went through a brutal court divorce. It
would be a good change of pace for her to start
over here in Florida."

"How does Georgette feel about the arrangement?"

"It is not an arrangement; it is a sound business
relationship," Jeffrey tried to clear up any miscon-
ception. "I haven't been cheating on my wife; nor
do I have any plans of sleeping around with Velma."

"I never said that you were having an affair."

"You insinuated that perhaps I would."

"Tell me. Is she good looking?" Dexter jokingly pried, as he reeled in the first catch of the day."

"The woman is fine. When it comes to her looks, she has the full package. Velma is stacked with the perfect bodily dimensions. We have a professional relationship except for her occasional flirting."

"Maybe there is something you have not picked up on."

"What are you saying?"

"Her actions may be intentional. Why else would she have jumped at your request to join you here in Orlando?

"Don't be silly." Jeffrey flatly laughed. "That doesn't make any sense."

"What other reason could there be for her willingness to make a long distance move to work with you on an unproven venture. I am going to ask you again. Have you mentioned Velma's impending move to Georgette? It probably will set off a red flag in your wife's mind even if Velma is not your mistress."

"No. I have not. You are over analyzing the situation. Georgette doesn't have anything to worry about."

"I know how condescending women can be from my own experience. I also know how easy it is for the right woman to break down a man defenses to get him into her clutches. You will see once Velma is here in Orlando. The woman is no longer married. You have invited her to follow you to Orlando. Georgette needs to be concerned about holding on to her man."

"My mother met Velma during our last company picnic and thinks very highly of her as a person. But that doesn't mean anything; she has never liked Georgette."

"Why are you telling me this?"

"I was merely sharing my mother's feeling about Velma."

Dexter relocated the boat to another spot near an artificial reef hoping to find a larger school of fish. He shifted gears on the boat grinding it to a halt. The buddies fished until late into the evening; ending up with a cooler filled with a variety of fish mostly sea bass, perch, and red snapper.

"I promised Georgette's mother if I had a large enough catch that we would have a family fish fry. You should join us. We will meet tomorrow at a little community park near downtown."

"I know for a fact, I can't be there. I have other plans. You should take my mess of fish. Tell the family I'm sorry, I could not attend."

A waterspout appeared out over the bristling Atlantic Ocean once they were back on shore. Rain roared in from the distant horizon as the men scurried to leave.

The outdoorsmen would have many similar outings in the coming years.


The next afternoon as planned Jeffrey, Georgette and her family met in the park.

A celebration swung into action at the onset of the fish fry. It took Marjorie completely off guard. Immersed in conversation with Georgette, she failed to notice her mother lighting a cake in honor of her Thirty-first birthday. Susan tapped her older daughter on the back. She turned around to look. "Surprise! Happy birthday!" Everyone shouted in unison.

"Thank you," Marjorie said graciously. "You guys are the greatest. My birthday is a couple of days from now." She smiled and then blew out the candles on the cake."

"We will all be flying out of town in the morning," Georgette remarked.

"A family gathering in the park provided a perfect opportunity for us all to share in advance your special day," Susan added as she put an arm around Marjorie's shoulders.

"I know this was your idea, mom."

"The birthday idea was mine but the fish fry was Jeffrey's. I have to credit Jeffrey and his friend Dexter for the fish. Yesterday they had a successful fishing outing down in Jensen Beach."

"Dexter should have joined us."

"Well Marjorie, Dexter wanted to attend but he had a prior commitment," Jeffrey relayed Dexter's apology.

"You have been living without family here in Central Florida every since you finished college," Susan said setting up her question to follow. "What do you think about Georgette and Jeffrey moving to Orlando?"

"Georgette and I had always been close until I moved away to further my education."

"Think about it this way, Jeffrey and I will be flying back to Chicago and upon our return we will be here to stay," Georgette said in response to her half sister's emotional reply.

The following morning Georgette, Jeffrey as well as her mom, and stepfather boarded their flights out of town. Marjorie took time away from Alma Francis Community Clinic where she worked as a pediatric nurse to see them off.

## Chapter 6

Devon's office door was shut as he worked late preparing his next sermon when he heard a faint knock. Devon glanced at the door as it slowly opened. "Sister Trina Johnson, you're still here," Devon spoke as he got up from his desk to greet one of his most loyal members.

"I would have been gone if I hadn't stuck around to call my fellow women ministry members to remind them of our next meeting, which we will strategize how best to help the local needy population."

"That's wonderful, Trina. I can't help but ...."

"Devon shut up!" She demanded as she slipped out of her shoes."

He watched intensely as she pushed down on her skirt gliding it gracefully down her legs. Devon locked the door as she finished disrobing. Suddenly he felt short of breath. Trina strolled over to Devon and then proceeded to help him with the removal of his shirt and then slacks. Again he had fallen sway to the evils of the flesh. Trina was one of a half dozen women within the general population of the church romantically involved with the young minister. Walking out of his office, forty-five minutes later, tucking her blouse back into her cardigan skirt, she spotted the pastor's personal assistant still sitting at her desk.

"Ms. James, I thought you had left for tonight."

"I had stepped out briefly for a bite to eat. I am trying to catch up on my work since I am going to be out of town for the next three days."

"Try not to work too hard."

"Are you okay?" Ms. James spoke out of concern.

"I have been going through some trying times. That is why I dropped in on Pastor Tucker for spiritual guidance."

"I understand, Trina. Tell your mom I said hi."

Devon came out of his office as Trina proceeded on her way.

Ms. James turned her attention to Devon as he approached her workstation. "Pastor Tucker, you appear to have lipstick on your shirt collar and on your left cheek."

"I must have gotten a little too close to Sister Johnson while comforting and providing her personal counseling."

Ms. James smiled and laughed under her breath. "You don't have to explain your actions to me. Your fiancée on the other hand, if she was here, she would likely be concerned."

"We wouldn't want our members to get the wrong Idea! Since nothing happened!"

Ms. James detected harshness in Devon's voice. "Don't worry, honey. My lips are shut."

"Good. I'm glad, you see things my way."

"You don't have to answer to me." Ms. James shook her head. "But you will have to answer to the Lord."

"Do not forget to lockup on your way out. I will see you in a few days. Enjoy your time off."

"And I hope you have a good time at the young adults retreat in Daytona Beach. Devon, I understand you reluctantly accepted their offer to accompany them on their annual outing."

"As the future of our wonderful church the young people deserve to be supported," Devon said.

"I couldn't agree more," Ms. James said gracefully. "Give my best regards to Kim. Hopefully, she will get to be our next first lady."

## Chapter 7

Georgette's cell phone rang as her and Jeffrey finished packing the last of their belongings for their transition to Orlando.

"Hi Sister Bradbury, I'm Darlene Ricks the Chairman of the Assistance Minister Advisory Selection Committee; I have some information that I'd like to share."

"Hi Sister Ricks, I hope you're not the bearer of bad news."

"The reason for my call is actually to the contrary. After a thorough consideration of all candidates and the congregation's input we would like to offer you the position to be True Life Divinity's Assistant Pastor."

"I'm honored. I do not know what else to say, except thank you. Your timing could not have been better. Jeffrey and I are waiting on the movers."

"Great. We look forward to seeing you in a few days. We would like to go over the contract that you would be making with the church."

"Again I would like to say thanks. I'll touch base with you as soon as I arrive in Orlando."

"Tell Jeffrey hi."

Georgette glanced at Jeffrey. "Sister Ricks said hi." He smiled without uttering a word.

Rapping up her call, Georgette danced a quick gospel two-step.

"I haven't seen you this happy in a long, long time," Jeffrey acknowledged.

"Mrs. Ricks was calling from Orlando. Your wife is going to be the new Assistant Minister for True Life Divinity."

Jeffrey held her close in a tight embrace. He landed a kiss upon her lips. "After we send the movers on their way, we should still have time for dinner. I think we should celebrate your good news."

"Okay Jeff, but I'm going to choose the restaurant. Dinner at Captain Mike's Atlantic Fishery would be nice."

Jeffrey knew the high-end seafood establishment would require a reservation. "I'll give them a call to see if they will be able to accommodate us."

At the restaurant Jeffrey mentioned a couple of his employees that worked with him at the car dealership in Chicago would be joining him in Florida.

"These employees must be really special."

"They are extremely talented that's the reason I have chosen them to help out in the upstart of my deep sea fishing operation."

Georgette and Jeffrey went straight to the airport following dinner, shortly thereafter; they boarded a flight to Orlando to stay at a timeshare apartment for a few days before moving into their new home.

## Chapter 8

One week after Georgette officially signed off on her agreement with True Life Divinity to be their new assistant pastor; the Bradbury's hosted a house warming party. In attendance were family, friends, and The Bangor's Island Community Welcoming Committee.

"Georgette, if you have a moment, there's someone I would like for you to meet." Jeffrey spoke as she drew near.

"Yes dear," she responded with a smile on her face.

"I would like to introduce you to Herschel Foster a potential business associate. Herschel this is my lovely wife Georgette."

"Hi Herschel, it's nice to meet you."

"Hi. You are as lovely as I envisioned." Feeling compelled he spoke from his heart. "Jeffrey speaks very highly of you."

"Herschel is spearheading the effort to launch our river cruise venture."

"That's nice, gentlemen. If you will excuse me, I must greet my mother, and half sister; they just arrived."

The guys continued with their own conversation. "Dennison is still mulling over our financial proposition," Herschel stated."

"I wish he would make a decision," Jeffrey said. "I'm looking forward to our meeting with him on Monday. The fate of the whole operation hinges on having him as a major stakeholder."

"Unfortunately, we will have to reschedule. About an hour ago, Dennison left me a voice mail message that his attorney needs more time."

"Why would he need more time?" Jeffrey asked.

"He need more time to assess the risk involved. I guess we will have to hang tight."

Jeffrey watched Georgette as she headed over to the bar adjacent to the kitchen where Marjorie was seated. Their parents entered into a separate enclosed dining area, where a full buffet had been catered.

Georgette taped Marjorie on the shoulder. "Hi sis, I see you found your favorite spot."

Inez Maxwell brushed against Georgette as she walked past before Marjorie had a chance to respond. "Georgette, I'm sorry to have interrupted your conversation."

"No problem. Inez this is my half sister Marjorie. Inez is the president of our home owner's association."

"I know we met a few minutes ago." Marjorie raised her goblet to take a sip of wine.

"Did she also tell you that she is looking for a church home?"

"No." Marjorie answered nonchalantly.

"I have invited Inez to fellowship with us on Sunday."

"Lord knows I definitely need his covering." Inez's down trotting spirit could be felt as she shared her misfortunes. "I lost my husband in a horrible car accident just months ago after I was diagnosed with cervical cancer."

"You must be devastated," Marjorie replied.

"I am a broken soul. I'm going to call it a night. Look for me at church tomorrow."

Georgette and Jeffrey's house warming concluded two hours later as the last of their guest bade them goodnight.

## Chapter 9

Sunday morning, Minister Tucker opened up the doors to the church. As the choir sang, Inez Maxwell made her way toward the front of the church. Sitting in the pulpit Georgette nodded her head acknowledging Inez's decision in giving her life to the Lord. Jeffrey too had expressed an interest in joining True Life Divinity. However, Georgette never expected it would be that morning, which Jeffrey would also answer the Minister's call.

Following the service, as Georgette and Jeffrey were making their way through the parking area, Devon called out to them.

"Mr. and Mrs. Bradbury, I would like to have a moment of your time?"

"Of course, Minister Tucker, how may we help you?" Jeffrey asked.

"We should address each other on a first name basis as your lovely wife and I do."

"Okay, Devon."

The minister sought Jeffrey's immediate involvement in the church. "We have a vast array of ministries here at True Life of which you could select from to use your wealth of knowledge and talents."

"Perhaps I'll join the Men's Ministry."

"That would be ideal," Devon replied. The young adult males in our congregation are always in need of dynamic role models. I am sure Georgette would agree."

"Jeffrey and I are always supportive of each other in whatever we do."

"I head the Men's Ministry. The guys and I will be meeting this Wednesday at 7:00," Devon noted."

"If nothing unexpected arises, I'll be there." Jeffrey let his intention be known.

"Jeffrey that is wonderful. I will not hold you and the Mrs. any longer. Enjoy your day."

The next afternoon, Georgette had a talk with the Women's Ministry President Barbara Renee Bassett about an upcoming meeting between the ministry heads. The Deacon Board called for the meeting to discuss how to deal with the allegations of their pastor being accused of adulterous behavior with female members of the congregation.

Barbara leaned forward sitting at Georgette's Desk. "I know the news has to be disturbing to you as our new assistant pastor. However, Georgette this isn't the first time the church has had to deal with Pastor Tucker regarding this issue."

"What prompted the discussion previously?" Georgette questioned.

"Oh. It went beyond discussion. He was subjected to a church recall vote a few years ago."

"He shouldn't expect any leniency with his credibility still tarnished," Georgette implied. "I am surprised the church took on someone unmarried as their minister anyway."

"When he became minister he was married," Barbara emphasized. "His marriage didn't survive all the talk of him being an adulterer."

"Hopefully, verifiable evidence will be presented this time to substantiate his alleged infidelity." Georgette said. "I'm really sorry for his fiancée, Kim."

"I'm not," Barbara shot back. She was a member of the church before when all hell broke loose."

"You can't be serious," Georgette expressed disbelief.

"I'm dead serious. Nevertheless we should go into the meeting with an open mind on Saturday."

# Eddie Johnson

"You are right," Georgette agreed. "We should pray to the Lord and allow him to guide us in taking action if warranted."

Barbara reached for her purse while standing to her feet. "My husband has planned our night out. And with that being said, I'm leaving."

## Chapter 10

Georgette arrived home to find her husband glued to the television watching a cable sports channel.

"Hi Georgette, you're home early."

"Having had enough already for one day, I decided to cut out after our finance committee meeting."

He got up, walked over to Georgette, and then greeted her with a kiss.

"Finance Chairman William Dirksen announced my husband once again provided the church with a generous donation. I was thoroughly in awe. The committee members said they cannot thank you enough for your gift of love."

"You should know me by now. I always try to do what's right."

"I remember telling you how much the church needed to pay off its current debt and to start preliminary planning for a new envisioned place of worship; but I never intended for you foot the entire bill," Georgette responded.

"It's not like they had a lot remaining to pay," Jeffrey said. "I'm sure you would agree; God blesses us so that we can be a blessing to others."

Twenty-four hours later, Jeffrey would attend his first Men's Ministry meeting.

On the agenda was a mentoring program where members were given a volunteer opportunity to help male youth within the congregation to grow academically, spiritually, and socially.

As the plea went out a list was circulated for those wanting to sign up for the cause.

Devon acting in his role as chairman of the Males in Action Ministry introduced Jeffrey as a newcomer.

"I cannot think of a better use of free time than to devote it in helping our young brethren," Jeffrey boldly asserted.

"Let us give our new brother Jeffrey Bradbury a hand," Minister Tucker asked as he led them in a rousing hand of applause. "Brother Bradbury has the total package. He is a living testimony of a Christian living a full life in the business arena and at home. We should be grateful that the Lord has sent him to be a part of our church family."

Jeffrey would select Antonio Richards a high school teenager as his mentee.

## Chapter 11

Deacon Board Chairman Brandon Roberts called to order the Minister's Disciplinary Investigation Committee meeting. Sister Bassett presented to the chairman a list of women within the congregation of which Minister Tucker was accused of having inappropriate sexual relations. Deacon Johnson's wife Trina was at the top of the list.

Sister Darlene Ricks spoke first. "Amelia James our minister's personal assistant said she noticed Sister Trina Johnson exiting Minister Tucker's office straightening her disheveled clothing on several occasions late at night when she thought everyone had left. Sister James recalled one instance in which Minister Tucker had lipstick on his cheek and shirt collar following one of the visits by Sis Trina."

"How did Minister Tucker explain their actions?"

"He said that he was counseling Sis Trina who was going through hard times."

Next on the agenda was a cell phone video taken by an anonymous source showing Minister Tucker and the Young Adult Ministry President Carlotta Sands engaging in inappropriate touching while exchanging flirtatious remarks at a recent church outing in Daytona Beach. The two had come upon each other after wondering off down the shoreline.

Georgette moved her head from side to side displaying a look of disgust.

The committee moved on to discuss the other two young ladies on the list that was caught alone with the minister at his friend Douglas Allen's beach house. Sister Basset would provide the details. "Mrs. Allen walked in on Minister Tucker in a sexually compromising position with parishioner Sabrina Davis while her friend Jackie Edwards observed," Sister Bassett blurted setting off a flurry of commotion amongst the committee.

"Would Mrs. Allen be willing to testify as to what she witnessed at the beach house," Sister Ricks lashed out."

"I have already asked and she would be willing," Sister Bassett answered.

The Chairman entertained a motion that was accepted and unanimously approved setting up a recall vote to take place a week after the church's Caribbean cruise.

Georgette would pay Marjorie a visit at home. She would fill her in on the outcome of Minister Tucker's disciplinary hearing.

"There could be a positive outcome…"

"I do not follow your reasoning," Georgette wanted her to finish speaking."

"Are you serious?" Marjorie exclaimed. "I should not have to spell it out."

"You were implying something before you stopped in mid sentence."

"Once Devon is kicked out as minister the door will be open for you. There you have it."

"My goal is to one-day head my own congregation," Georgette acknowledged.

"This could be your perfect opportunity. Don't blow your chance. You should at least try. Give it your best shot."

"But I don't have enough experience."

"You have more than a little theological training. You graduated in the top tier of your seminary class."

"I'm referring to real life ministry experience," Georgette countered. "People are judged on what they bring to the table; if you know what I mean."

"The work you have done since graduating has been stupendous."

"How did you come to that conclusion?" Georgette asked. "Please let me know."

"You preached at your dad's church as youth pastor for over two years. And since moving to Orlando you have excelled in your role as True Life Divinity's Assistant Minister."

"Thanks for the words of encouragement. Perhaps I should give it further thought."

"Don't think too hard," Marjorie advised. "I cannot think of anyone else more deserving. This could be your time to shine."

"Marjorie, you may be right."

"I am right. Devon's downfall could be your blessing."

"A major decision like this should only be made once I have thought it through thoroughly."

## Chapter 12

Ms. James buzzed Georgette's office. "Yes, Ms. James,"

"You have a visitor. Her name is Debra Atkinson. She introduced herself as an old acquaintance of yours from Jersey City."

"Tell Ms. Atkinson I'll be right out."

"Alright, I'll let her know."

"Mrs. Bradbury will be right with you. You may have a seat."

Debra picked up a brochure from Ms. James desk detailing their upcoming Caribbean cruise.

"You're welcome to join us." Ms. James spoke. We should be setting sail in a few weeks. If you are interested let me know. And to give those a chance to go who cannot afford it, we will be raffling off 10 tickets."

Georgette walked out into the waiting area. "Debra it has been quite awhile since we last met."

The two women shared a friendly hug.

"How are you doing?" Georgette paused for a response that would not be forthcoming. "I was about to leave for lunch. Would you like to join me?"

"I really don't think that would be necessary. However, I would like to talk with you in private."

"Sure. Why don't you follow me back to my office?"

"Okay."

The ladies remained silent on the way back.

"You have a lovely office." Debra said as she took a seat across the desk from Georgette.

"Thank you. Don't tell me you traveled all the way from Jersey to see me."

"No. Unlike you, I never finished my ministerial training. I fell on hard times and ended up here in Orlando after being laid off from work. I thought by moving to Central Florida I would better my chances of landing a new job. Within a few weeks of making the move, I became homeless. I am still struggling years later working two jobs just to make ends meet."

"Debra. How may I help you? True Life Divinity has a pantry if you are in need of food. We also have a voucher program if you need help with your bills."

"I don't want your church handout. I have a more lucrative proposition, which I hope you will entertain. I would like for you to provide me with two hundred and fifty thousand dollars."

"A friend would not make that kind of demand. Debra you cannot be serious; you are trying to play a practical joke on me."

"If I do not have the funds within a specified time, I will request a meeting with your Deacon Board. I'll inform them that your were impregnated by a young minister while attending Jersey City Seminary and that he paid to have the fetus aborted."

"I don't have that kind of money at my disposal."

"Your filthy rich husband is loaded with cash," Debra sarcastically implied.

"My only bank account is a joint account with my husband. How could you be so ruthless?"

"I'm tired of never succeeding. You never struggled a day in your life. You can't relate to my plight!" Debra picked up a pen and started writing on Georgette's desk calendar.

"What are you doing?"

"The last day you have to provide me with the money is the 15th of next month. I wrote the date and my phone number on your calendar." Debra stood to her feet. "Have a nice lunch. I'll see myself out."


Georgette dialed Jersey City minister Thomas Miles. His secretary buzzed his office.

"Yes, Ms. Penelope."

"Pick up on line one; you have a call from a Mrs. Georgette Bradbury from Orlando."

"Hi Mrs. Bradbury, what shall I say would be the reason for this call?"

"I know you probably thought you would never hear from me again, however, we need to talk," Georgette promptly responded.

"Sure. I may have a few minutes to spare."

"Okay. First let me say, I am the new assistant minister of True Life Divinity Baptist Church in Orlando."

"Congratulation, I knew you would find a way to make a difference somewhere in ministry."

"Thank you."

"I still remember vividly the sweltering hot summer at seminary," Thomas spoke as he typed away on his computer. "I was on campus conducting a workshop."

"You introduced yourself and we went out to dinner," Georgette reminisced. "Afterwards, you took me back to my off campus apartment; I looked in my purse for my keys, and realized that I was locked out."

"That's when I took you to my extended stay hotel room to hang out until your roommate returned." Thomas interjected.

"The slick talking minister had me in bed no sooner than the door could slam shut."

"Georgette, we should not dwell on that part of our past? What ever happened that night should have never taken place. You and I have since married."

"Our professional careers could be in jeopardy," Thomas' old friend said with a slight tremble in her voice.

His heart sank. Thomas knew the crux of what she would be saying next; somehow their dreaded past was now coming back to haunt them. He closed his eyes, shaking his head, waiting for her to confirm his worst fear.

"I had an unexpected visit from someone I thought was a friend who only minutes ago left my office. Do you remember Debra Atkinson?"

"Yes. She was your off campus roommate I eluded to earlier."

"She has demanded that I provide her with two hundred and fifty thousand dollars. If I don't come up with the money she will reveal to my church's Deacon Board that you impregnated me and that you paid a clinic to abort the fetus."

"Oh no, I wish I could do something...," He stopped talking in mid sentence. "My church is struggling financially and my home is on the brink of foreclosure."

"Don't worry about it. I do not expect you to help. I will take care of everything. The reason for my call is to make you aware of Debra's action to manipulate us for her own personal gain. If word should get back to your congregation of this fiasco it could signal an end to you being pastor of Blessed Truth."

"I agree. How could Debra be so heartless?"

"That only puts it mildly. Other unrighteous words could sum up her behavior."

"The two of you were close friends at seminary. At least I thought you were."

"I have nothing further to say," Georgette said. "I'll pray for our lives to get better. I will keep you posted.

## *Chapter 13*

Velma arrived at Jeff's Deep Sea Fishing weeks in advance of its opening. Jeffrey's office manager in charge of booking fishing expeditions and front desk operations was ready for her new challenge. A cool morning breeze was blowing. The morning high tide lapped the shoreline as she parked her vehicle. She raised the top on her convertible, exited the vehicle, walked over to the establishment, and pulled the side door. It opened. "Hello! Jeff, I'm here!" She yelled.

Jeffrey emerged from a hallway to the right of the front counter. "Hi Velma, I didn't expect to see you until later."

"I couldn't wait to get started. So here I am."

"Come with me to your new office."

The first door down the hallway to the left had her name and title affixed. Velma entered and noticed a bouquet of fresh red roses on the desk.

"Wow, Jeffrey the flowers are lovely," she exclaimed.

"I hope you will accept them as a token of my gratitude for you being such a special person."

"I'll gladly accept any gifts from my man."

"One day you are going to stop flirting."

"Maybe, one day I'll get the man of my dreams." She walked over to the desk and removed the card attached to the flowers. The woman that followed him all the way from Chicago was no longer dressed in her usual business attire. She was noticeably relaxed as she stood in a low cut tank top blouse pulled over a pair of faded blue jeans. Velma read the words aloud from the card, which Jeffrey had so eloquently written as she gently spun around to face him. The smile on her face said to Jeffrey that she was going to be more than happy in her new position. "I need to get situated. Afterwards, I would like to go over to the nearby shopping center to stock up on office supplies."

"Remind me before you leave I have a business credit card for your use."

Jeffrey treated Velma to a local deli for lunch.

"You are going to spoil a girl. I was surprised with flowers and now lunch. I am flattered."

"Don't expect this to be the norm. I wanted your first day to be special. So how is the food?"

"The hoagie ranks amongst the best I have had and I the love special house flavored drink."

"Georgette and I seldom eat out. She is a very busy woman."

Jeffrey's response provided Velma an opening for a question she had been itching to ask. "How are you and the Mrs. doing?"

"Why would you ask? We are fine."

"You have the ideal marriage."

"We have the right chemistry that keeps us together, a major part of which is our Christian faith."

"My marriage started out the same way until we grew about apart over time and then it abruptly ended." Distraught she gasped for air. "The bastard had been having an affair for several years. That explained why our relationship kept deteriorating."

"Would your move to Orlando have anything to do with trying to start over?" Jeffrey quizzed.

"To some extent it probably played into my decision." Velma appeared to wipe tears from her eyes with her free hand. "I still wake up at night crying my heart out alone in bed. My husband divorced me after 15 years for a younger."

Jeffrey and his sidekick returned to the office to resume preparation for his business opening.

# Temptation in the Pulpit

*Chapter 14*

A sold out cruise liner at dusk departed the Cape
Canaveral's Space Coast embarking on a seven day
whirl wind tours of various Caribbean ports of call.
Most notable of these locales would be the Grand
Cayman Island and Cozumel.

On board the ship was a large group of True Life
Divinity Baptist Church parishioners, families, and
friends.

During dinner on the first night, Georgette, Marjorie, Susan and Carlton were entertained by Minister Devon Tucker and his leading lady Kim.
Georgette sensed Devon did not have a clue of his
looming ouster from the church.

Leaving the dining hall, Georgette waved to her
parents who were heading back to their cabin, as
she rushed to join Marjorie entering the elevator on
their way to the ninth floor comedy club.

Debra Atkinson boarded the elevator on the
eighth floor. The demented soul eyed Georgette
squarely in the face. "Don't forget our deal minister
Bradbury," Debra snidely remarked.

"Please do not make me lose my religion!
Georgette shouted. "I am on vacation with my

family! I can do without your nonsense!" She thought to herself, fuming, and gesturing wildly with her hands. How did the devil manage to get onboard?

Getting off on the ninth floor the sisters walked briskly trying not to miss the introduction of the first comedic act.

"The woman in the elevator hit a nerve with you," Marjorie verbalized her observation. "You seem shaken."

"I'm fine. We'll talk about it later." The laughter within the club calmed her tattered nerves.

In the morning, Georgette and her family met for breakfast on the lower deck.

"I need some motherly advice," Georgette said after sipping on her coffee. "Devon may be relieved as pastor. Although, I would hate to see him go it could be an opportunity for me."

"It seems like a no brainer to me. You should go for it. However, since your father is a minister perhaps you should get his opinion."

"Your mother is right. His downfall may be your foot in the door. Let me guess. Devon has given into the evils of the flesh. He is constantly tempted by women and they are often tempted by him. Many ministers have fallen from grace due to the opposite sex."

"You are right dad. How could you have known? Devon is sexually involved with several young women from True Life Divinity and will be voted out as minister once we are back in Orlando."

"How can you be so certain?" Susan asked.

"I'm on the disciplinary committee that has reviewed the irrefutable evidence which will result in his ouster."

"There is something else Georgette should share. A woman traveling with us on the cruise is threatening to have her removed as assistant minister. Georgette and I have discussed her devious extortion plot. Last night I got to see the Jezebel up close."

"Hush child! Be careful of what you speak into the wind. That cannot be true."

"She is right mom. The woman knows about my not so perfect past. Her name is Debra Atkinson. You probably remember her as my roommate from seminary. Debra knows I terminated my ill-fated pregnancy."

"You cannot let her get away with destroying everything that you worked so hard to attain."

"It's not like I have a choice. I will have to give into her demand."

"What are you saying?" Georgette's father asked firmly.

"If I do not provide her with two hundred and fifty thousand dollars she will tell the Deacon Board about the abortion."

"You should not allow yourself to be manipulated. We as ministers are always talking about spiritual warfare. I think the time is right for a battle. I am going to pray to the Lord to guide you in overcoming this obstacle." Minister Hatcher and family stood around the table with their heads bowed and their hands joined as his prayer went up to Heaven.

The cruise ship arrived in the Cayman Islands. On Grand Cayman, the largest island in the chain, within their shore-time, Amelia James would have a beachside wedding. Ms. James would wed Sid Jackson a successful financial planner.

A picturesque wedding reception took place afterwards right on the beach.

# Eddie Johnson

The couple jumped the broom and then strutted their stuff on a hardwood makeshift floor; dazzling onlookers with an unexpected traditional ballroom style of dancing performing the Jitterbug and the Charleston.

Minister Tucker provided a few words of guidance for the newlyweds. "Marriage should not be taking lightly. It should be built on trust and the understanding of each other's needs."

An elderly frail member within the church entourage commented. "Minister Tucker should know. He learned the lesson the hard way." Minister Tucker stopped speaking until the woman finished her poorly timed assault on his character and for the crowd riled up by her insensitivity to quiet. He went on to wish the couple a great life together.

Meanwhile onshore in Orlando, Jeffrey took Velma up on her offer to have dinner at a local Italian restaurant. Their night out was to celebrate the upcoming opening of his company Jeff's Deep Sea Fishing. Velma's intentions were clear to Jeffrey although he pretended not to be aware. "How is your mother? The last time I saw her at the company picnic in Chicago she was quite a lively soul."

"That is putting her vivaciousness lightly; she's quite a remarkable woman for her age. Mother or Linda as she prefers to be called could not be better. Between the church groups and community volunteer organizations that she is affiliated with the woman is constantly on the go."

"I would like to have a party for our employees near the end of the year around the holidays."

Velma volunteered to coordinate the outing. "I'll make sure it happens by putting it on my list of things to do. I hope your wife attends. We should get to know each other."

The two talked non-stop even after finishing their meal until closing time for the restaurant.


Around midnight the cruise ship pulled into Cozumel the last port of call on their itinerary.

The morning found vacationers enjoying its sandy beaches.

Georgette and Marjorie would venture into town shopping for souvenir trinkets to remember their stopover in the Mexican seaside town. "I hope Jeffrey likes these leisure shorts and Cozumel slogan tees."

"You could have asked him if he would have accompanied you."

"I'm fine with his decision not to come. He has a new business to launch."

"That's why some marriages fail when a partner starts thinking more about his or her work than their spouse."

"Maybe you will find your own Christian mate before we return to Central Florida."

"I get the hint. You want me to butt out of your personal life."

"Thank you."

The following night the cruise liner was en route back to Florida.

Marjorie was having trouble sleeping so she visited an all night food court to grab a cup of coffee. Sitting at a table alone looking out over the choppy waters of the darkened sea she was approached by a dapper black brother who walked over and introduced himself.

"Hi. I am Brian Dickson. You look lonely. Would you mind if I join you."

"Hi Brian. Please have a seat. I am Marjorie Stevens."

"I know. You are Minister Bradbury's half sister."

"So you are a member of True Life Divinity."

"Yes. Your brother in law Jeffrey recently joined our church family." Brian observed Marjorie's pleasant smile. "I wanted to approach you. I just didn't have the nerve."

"Brian. I have quite an intimidating persona."

"You remind me a lot of my mother."

"I never have been told that before," Marjorie said putting an emphasis on every syllable." How do I remind you of the lady of whom you care so deeply?"

"She was reared in a family headed by an influential male preacher too. And like you, she was often overshadowed by her younger female sibling."

"I have never felt over shadowed by Georgette. We have chosen different careers. She is a successful assistant minister and I'm a successful pediatric nurse at a local community clinic."

"I guess my perception was wrong."

"Do you have any younger brothers are sisters."

"You are going to find this quite amusing. My father was a highly respected electrical engineer in the local area. He died a few years ago."

"I'm sorry. I fail to see the humor in the passing of your father."

"I said that to say this, my mother has since re-married. Two months into the marriage she be-came pregnant and now I have a two month old half brother."

"You will be more like his uncle."

"I know. Isn't that something? I hope they're up to the challenge of rearing a young child at their late age."

"I'm quite sure they'll do just fine. Most likely your half brother will have some of your traits and that will bode well for him."

"This may sound crazy. Although we have just met, you seem like someone I've known my entire life."

"Okay Brian. It's getting really thick; you're go-ing to need a shovel to dig your way out."

"And you have a nice sense of humor to boot."

The two continued sharing each other's company for the remainder of the cruise.

## Chapter 15

Georgette walked through the church doors stopping briefly at Ms. James desk for a brief chat before starting her day.

"How are you this morning, Minister Bradbury."

"I'm fine. And how are you."

"I am buried under a mountain of paperwork as usual. Otherwise, I'm good."

"Having work is a good thing.

While at sea I had a long talk with your friend from seminary."

"You must be referring to Debra. Did she say anything that would be of interest?" Georgette asked.

"Debra is looking forward to being a member of True Life Divinity."

"You can't be serious."

"Why would I lie? You have always been joyous when I have mentioned souls wanting to give their lives to the Lord. Why should Ms. Debra be any different?

"To understand how I feel about Debra, you would have to know her on a more personal level."

"She appears to be a nice person."

"Rededicating her life to God is probably the last thing on her mind. How on earth did she ever end up on the cruise?"

"I guess you forgot we raffled off tickets for the cruise. Debra was the lucky recipient of two of the tickets. She brought a male friend along with her on the cruise with her extra ticket. He goes by the nickname Snake."

"Somehow that doesn't sound Christian like."

"I know," Ms. James agreed. "He seems to be quite worldly."

"Devon will be meeting with the Deacon Board this afternoon. He will be informed of allegations lodged against him and his impending recall."

"I wonder how he will respond to the news."

"He'll probably be devastated. But you always reap what you sow in the end."

"Amen, sister."

Clueless and thirty minutes late, Minister Tucker appeared before the Deacon Board.

A sane person should have been more subdued. "Be prepared if you follow through with this charade and wrongfully remove me from my position, I will sue you in court!" Devon ranted defiantly. "You should get the best legal representation possible! You will need it! Am I clear?" He slammed both of his hands down on the table.

"We understand you are under pressure," Chairman Roberts asserted. "Your inexcusable rude behavior will not be tolerated. You have been informed of our intentions. Those in favor of Minister Tucker being asked to leave the meeting should let it be known by a show of hands."

Devon would leave without saying another word.

Georgette having sat in on the meeting observed firsthand the unfortunate calamity. "I can't believe what we witnessed," she voiced her displeasure. "He's clearly in denial of the facts that were presented."

After taking care of the remaining items on the agenda, Chairman Roberts dismissed the meeting.

## Chapter 16

Jeffrey visited with Tonya Richards and her son Antonio at their apartment in a multi-unit housing complex in the Paramore Neighborhood of Orlando. Tonya greeted her guest and then invited him into their modest living quarters. "Have a seat," Tonya said with a smile. "Thank you for coming." She struck up a conversation. "Antonio should be a star basketball player on his school's basketball team this year after a stellar performance last season. He attends Stedman Miller High a new private charter school here on the west side of the city. Antonio's ball handling skills may be the missing ingredient the Black Bears need to compete for a state championship.

"How are you, Antonio?"

"I am doing fine," he said grumpily as the muscles in his face tightened.

"Your mother informed me that you are struggling with your studies. She said you probably could use help with your Calculus and Civic classes. You are obviously a bright young man."

"You don't know anything about me!" The young man testily cried out.

"I would like to say, I am sorry that your father, a marine sergeant, recently passed."

"You're going to talk about my dad. You never knew him."

"I understand he died fighting in Afghanistan just as the war began winding down. My father also died when I was about your age in a car accident. While driving on the Kennedy Expressway in Chicago his car was rear ended by a dump truck. It careened out of control flipping several time before bursting into flames," Jeffrey spoke with a timeless sense of loss reflecting in his voice. "Your father would want you to improve your grades to be eligible to help your team. He did not raise a quitter."

"Are you done with your lecture?" Antonio spewed unwarranted bitterness.

"I'm not lecturing you. Should you truly need help with your studies, I am qualified to assist. If you need someone to talk with, I am here to listen, and to give practical advice. We can hang out on the weekends."

"He wished his father could have attended more of his basketball games," Tonya reflected back. "My work schedule also precluded me from making most of his games."

"If you stop slacking with your grades, which I believe you are, I'll try to attend all of your home and away games," Jeffrey vowed.

"Mr. Bradbury has a deep sea fishing business."

"I would love to have you accompany me on our initial deep sea fishing excursion. The company officially kicks off in a few weeks."

"I definitely will not stand in your way. My boy needs your help."

"I'm waiting for your answer, Antonio. What do say?

"Well, it could be fun," he replied glumly.

"We have a date. I will pick you up." Jeffrey and Antonio exchanged cell phone numbers. "I will text message you later in the week with the exact time to be ready."

Tonya walked Jeffrey out to his car.

"You are a really nice man. Maybe we can spend some time together."

"I do not swing that way!" Tonya detected anger and disgust in his voice. She hung her head as he objected to her uncanny suggestion. "I am here to help your son. I'm happily married to my wife who happens to be your assistant pastor."

"I missed spoke. I am not that kind of woman. Forgive me."

"I have forgiven you. When the time is right some lucky man will make his presence known to you."

Jeffrey watched a refreshed smile return to Tonya's face as he steered his vehicle away from the curb merging with traffic.

## Chapter 17

Jeffrey and Georgette waited at a traffic light near the entrance to True Life Divinity and noticed the parking lot at almost capacity. The couple had barely spoken on their way over.

He immediately parked once on the church grounds. "I'm surprise, most of the members are already here," Georgette, verbalized her observation as they were walking towards the church.

"I can imagine the commotion going on inside." Jeffrey surmised.

The parishioners were poised to hear the allegations against their pastor, which would enable them to make a decision on his fate.

"They're probably gossiping and speculating as to how something like this could happen." Georgette further noted.

Entering the vestibule of the sanctuary the noise level was more deafening than they could have anticipated. Marjorie was seated at the end of a pew midway of the church. Taking a break from chatting with Brian, she waved to Georgette and Jeffrey as they strolled by.

"I guess Brian is officially my half sister's new beau."

"How did you derive at that conclusion?"

"I can assure you it is much deeper than a buddy-buddy relationship. The two became acquainted during our church cruise. All Ms Marjorie talked about on our return to shore was the guy she met name Brian."

Jeffrey took a seat as Georgette proceeded on her way to the pulpit shaking hands along the way.

The Deacon Board was seated on their reserved front row pew. The Disciplinary Investigation Committee was seated directly behind them.

Deacon Board Chairman Brandon Roberts promptly called the special meeting to order. He recapped the reason for the recall vote and expounded on the seriousness of the allegations.

An elderly woman in the congregation stood to her feet screaming at the top of her lungs. "This ain't nothing but a sham! Y'all want to replace him with that young girl, Georgette Bradbury."

Parishioners became boisterous; fired up by her ill-timed opinion.

"Please, settle down," Brandon elevated his voice to maintain order. "Hold your comments or questions until we've covered all items on the agenda." After regaining control, he called Sister Bassett to the podium to present the committees finding against Minister Tucker.

Sister Bassett stood to her feet and then proceeded to stride gracefully to the front of the church. The bottom of her pleated maxi skirt swayed effortlessly. Facing the congregation, Sis Bassett acknowledged everyone, given special recognition to God and to those in the pulpit. She delivered the damaging information. "Finding number one: Minister Tucker had sexual relations with Mrs. Trina Johnson within his church office. Finding number two: Minister Tucker was caught on camera displaying inappropriate behavior flirting with the young adult ministry president Carlotta Sands during the auxiliary's recent Daytona Beach retreat. Finding number Three: Minister Tucker was also caught with parishioner Sabrina Davis at a beach house in Daytona Beach unclothed in a sexually promiscuous position, while her friend Jackie Edwards looked on."

The chairman called Amelia James, Minister Tucker's Personal Assistant to the podium.

## Temptation in the Pulpit

Ms. James willing and ready to speak hastily adjusted the microphone. "I witnessed Sis Trina frequenting the Minister's office on numerous occasions; she would leave with her clothing disheveled, and on one occasion he had lipstick on his cheek, and shirt collar. I tried to give him the benefit of the doubt, until the day I twisted the door and looked inside his office. I was shocked. He was having sex with Sis Trina." After making her brief statement, she returned to her seat.

Rhonda Allen would next tell her unfortunate revelation. "My husband Douglas gave Minister Tucker permission to use our beach house so he could get some much needed rest and relaxation. Having visited the house earlier, I had inadvertently left behind a manuscript on a thesis for one of my college classes. I opened the door to find Sabrina Davis stark naked with Minister Tucker partially disrobed hugging and kissing, while her scantily clad friend Jackie Edwards watched. Sabrina, Jackie, and the minister were oblivious to the fact I was observing, until I yelled for them to get out. When I told my husband about the incident, he suggested for the good of the church that I should not tell anyone. However, I am here today to say that type of

**77**

behavior will not be tolerated!" Ms. Allen shouted to the top of her lungs. "He should be relieved of his ministerial position!"

Chairman Roberts grabbed the microphone. "Mrs. Allen, please take your seat! You were not to convey your personal feelings!"

"I'm sorry." She threw both hands up into the air. "My emotions overruled my sanctity," she spoke as she sashayed on back to her seat.

The lights in the sanctuary dimmed. True Life members witnessed an edited cell phone video of their pastor and Carlotta Sands flirting and inappropriately touching at a recent Young Adult Ministry outing in Daytona Beach.

A question and answer session kicked off as the light were brought back up to full intensity.

A member asked about the legality of the recall vote. "It would be binding as long as wrongdoing could be proven. Minister Tucker nevertheless plans to file a civil lawsuit if ousted."

Ushers fanned throughout the vast edifice handing out ballots as the chairman provided an explanation on how to fill in the forms and to mark their entries. Ample time was given for everyone to make their selections and to cast their votes as they exited the sanctuary. The embattled minister's fate would not be announced until the following Sunday morning 2$^{nd}$ service.

## Chapter 18

Ms. James buzzed Georgette's phone. "Ms. Debra Atkinson is here to see you. She states it is regarding a business proposition."

Georgette thought to herself, I was expecting her today, but not this early in the morning. "Send her back," she instructed Ms. James and mumbled a few undecipherable words as she put down the phone.

"Follow the hallway to left and she will be in the first office on the right."

"Georgette's door was open as Debra strutted in and took a seat.

"I hope you got my money." Debra immediately sneered.

"Hell would freeze over before I give into your demand."

"Those are harsh words to be coming from a woman of the Lord."

"You on the other hand represent Satan. I will not stray away from the will of my God. He will direct my steps."

"I thought you would have provided me a better welcome. I'm going to give you more time to dwell on the consequences should you fail to act as instructed."

"No one owes you anything. The only difference between us is that I refused to let my misfortunes hold me back. Although, you did not finish your seminary training the Lord still cares for you."

"Go ahead preach, Georgette," Debra chided her once close friend.

"I don't have anything further to say. You should get out of my office!"

"Rumor has it that you desires to be the next minister of True Life. Tomorrow, Devon Tucker will be relieved of that position after the recall vote is made public."

"Stop rambling about Devon and make your point," Georgette growled.

"The amount needed to keep quiet about your illegitimate aborted fetus has just increased to five hundred thousand dollars."

"Woman, are you insane? You should not expect to get that kind of money from me or anyone."

"I'm not bluffing. If you want to further your ministerial career here at this marvelous church, you will find away to get the loot. I know how much your husband is worth." Debra rolled her eyes as she proceeded to taunt Georgette. "You never told him. He doesn't know."

"What doesn't he know?

"I don't believe you ever told your sweet husband Jeffrey about the abortion. He never knew you were impregnated by Minister Thomas Miles."

"Leave Thomas and his congregation out of this mess. They already have their hands full dealing with problems. You might as well leave. In case you did not hear me the first time, I do not intend to entertain your offer. I am not afraid to deal with my past. I have the Lord on my side."

"Remember you have two weeks to make the right decision if you would like to be True Life Divinity's next pastor. If you don't smart up I am going to have you removed from your seat in the pulpit."

Georgette venomously spewed out a slew of heated remarks. "I have nothing further to say! You should leave! There is the door! I suggest that you use it!" Georgette pointed a finger in the direction of the door.

## Chapter 19

Saturday morning, Herschel Foster rang the doorbell at the Bradbury's. "Good morning Mrs. Bradbury, I'm here to meet with Jeffrey."

"Good Morning. It's my understanding the two of you will be teeing off on the community golf course," Georgette said.

"That's right. Jeffrey has been bragging about his awesome game."

"He would like to prove his point."

"I guess. I'm surprise he is not ready."

"Have a seat. Jeffrey should be out shortly. I'll let him know you are here."

As Georgette turned to check on him, Jeffrey suddenly emerged from a nearby hallway carrying his golf gear ready to hit the course. Jeffrey would plant a kiss on his wife's lips prior to heading out the door with Herschel.

From the first hole of play, Herschel and Jeffrey reflected on their failure to gain the needed financial support for their much anticipated river cruise venture. "It was a grandiose idea but finding another investor in today's economy could prove nearly impossible," Jeffrey reasoned.

"Perhaps you are right. However, we should not give up that easy. We should continue our search for a replacement investor awhile longer."

It didn't take long before Herschel landed his ball in the rough. Jeffrey took an early lead.

"How are you doing with your deep sea fishing business?" Herschel inquired.

"Good. Our inaugural kickoff will be on next Saturday. My crew and I are just about done with the entire behind the scene readiness process."

"Are you still looking for investors?"

"Yes. In the interim while waiting to see if our river cruise venture will be revived, I would love you to consider investing in my little upstart company. You should come along for our initial business launch excursion."

"It's a great idea."

"So you will be on hand. I would love to have you as a guest."

"Well my plans could change. I will get back to you later in the week with a firm confirmation.

At the end of several holes, Herschel conceded to Jeffrey.

"You have more than proven your point. I suck at golf."

"That wasn't my intent. We were just having a knock around game."

"I should play more often."

## Chapter 20

True Life Divinity's congregation packed their sanctuary on a Sunday morning. The majority of the members appeared somber awaiting the results of the recall vote.

Georgette had been briefed beforehand of the outcome.

The service started as it usually did with praise and worship.

After the praise team failed to raise the spirits of those in the congregation, Deacon Brandon Roberts made his way to the podium. "Good morning church!" A few of the members responded. "I said good morning True Life Divinity!" Again, a lackluster response ensued. Deacon Roberts went forth with the information, which everyone had been awaiting. "Over ninety percent of the parishioners voted for the ouster of Minister Devon Tucker." He provided the final tally. "Our work is not done. We must now find a replacement for our troubled ex minister."

Georgette took to the pulpit delivering a rousing sermon connecting with the downtrodden. Souls were finally set on fire. The lady minister spoke on staying grounded in God's Word when fending off the evils of the world. She took her text from Psalm 27:1, 2 KJV. - The Lord is my light and my salvation; whom shall I fear? the Lord is the strength of my life; of whom shall I be afraid? 2 When the wicked, even mine enemies and my foes, came upon me to eat up my flesh, they stumbled and fell.

## Chapter 21

Georgette in support of her husband was on hand on a blustery Saturday morning for his inaugural deep sea-fishing trips. The company's two boats were ready and their crews were anxious to head out to sea. A local civic organization filled one of the boats. The other boat mostly carried invited guest, which included members of the community and fellow church members.

Jeffrey soon realized he did not have time to pick up Antonio. He would need to be on hand when the community group arrived. Pressed for time he dialed Tonya's cell phone. "Good Morning Mrs. Richards."

"Who is this? You're speaking with Tonya."

"I know. I am Jeffrey Bradbury. I promised your son Antonio that I would be taking him deep sea fishing."

"Where are you? My boy is waiting on you."

"We have a problem. I'm not going to be able to pick him up prior to our departure. I will have to be available to greet my first paid customers."

"You're lucky I am an understanding woman. However, my son on the other hand probably would not take so kindly to being stood up. Tell me where your place is located; and I'll bring him right over."

"Are you okay dear?" Georgette spoke as Jeffrey ended his call with Tonya.

"I had a slight problem; however, it has been resolved."

"From the look on your face I was beginning to worry," she stated while brushing back her hair. "Your friend Deacon Brandon Roberts and his son Randy have arrived."

Jeffrey turned his head to affirm his wife's observation. "His brother Deacon Seth Roberts is with them," he added.

Just as Brandon was parking his Jeep Cherokee a bus pulled into the driveway carrying the 'Oliver Simpson's Young Civic Leaders Association'. Jeffrey personally welcomed each member as he shook his or her hands while disembarking.

As Georgette finished greeting Brandon and Seth, Tonya Roberts tapped her on the shoulder. "Hi Tonya, I wasn't expecting you today."

"I'm fine. How are you? Your husband is mentoring my son Antonio."

"Will you be joining us?"

"No. I dropped off my son. Your husband Jeffrey was to pick him up but somehow he could not find the time."

"So being the great mom you are to help Jeffrey, you brought him over. Where is your young man?"

"Antonio is standing over by the water talking with a school mate."

"You are referring to my son Randy," Brandon butted into the conversation. "My son and I are fans of your son. I'm hoping my son also will try out for the school's basketball team."

"You are right, Randy should try," Tonya agreed. "I say that because his father Brandon Roberts used to be quite a good Georgia college basketball player. I never attended any of your games; I just kept up with you in the news. Unfortunately, you had a drug problem; otherwise, you probably would have made the pro draft."

"You don't have to remind me; I live each day with that memory. Growing up in poverty without a strong father figure I got in with a wrong crowd."

"A lot of young kids have vices," Tonya said. "I know I did. You got caught."

"Excuse me." Georgette interrupted their conversation. "It is time to board the boats. Everyone else appears to be ready."

"I guess Brandon and I got carried away talking." Tonya gave Brandon one last glance. "You look great. Tell your wife, I said hello. Enjoy."

Antonio would further acquaint himself with Tracy and his father Brandon as the boat pulled away from the shore. All signs of civilization including buildings eventually disappeared from the horizon as they went farther out to sea. Fifty to sixty miles offshore the boat grinded to a halt, straightaway everyone eagerly lowered their bated hooks into the seemingly endless abyss.

"My father used to marvel about you," Antonio stated as he turned his head to look at Brandon.

"Really?" Brandon replied.

"According to him you were a great college basketball player. I watched your son play at our local recreation center and in a few summer league games. Tracy is quite talented too."

"I think he is afraid of failing like his father did. Am I right son?"

"I have no comment," Randy answered flatly.

"You see what I mean. Maybe you can convince him to try out for your High school team. He is capable of playing every position on the court. At least, I think so. But I am bias, I am his father."

"You are knowledgeable of the game, so I respect your opinion Mr. Roberts."

"Tracy. I think you and Antonio could compliment each other quite well on the floor," Brandon added.

"Yeah Tracy, you should listen to your father. Why not try out for the team. You stand a better chance of being selected than some of the guys returning from last year."

"I have been pondering the idea," Tracy surprisingly said. "I'll make a decision soon."

"That's my boy." Brandon was pleased with his response; and it showed as he put an arm around him pulling him close.

Finally, one of the four caught a fish that was legal size allowing it to be kept.

"We've been throwing everything back and then Tracy lands a big one," Seth joked.

"We are definitely going to weigh this one," Crewmember Max Dean said while spearing the humungous sea bass assisting the young man in bringing it aboard. "A $100.00 reward will be given to the angler reeling in the largest fish." Others caught fish of comparable size as the day progressed.

On the way back, Jeffrey took control of the boat. Georgette sat in his lap with her hands on the wheel as he effortlessly guided the vessel back to its home dock.

A few minutes later, Jeffrey's other boat returned to shore. An announcement was made over the intercom that Tracy's large sea bass weighed 75 pounds. He came in second place to a young woman. She was also a first time deep-sea fisher. She had snagged a 107 pounds Tarpon.

Jeffrey let out a sigh of relief as he yawned. He watched as his guest made their way to their vehicles to depart his establishment. "I am glad you were on hand to share my opening day," he said with his eyes focused on his wife.

"Hopefully, we will not allow anybody or anything to ever come between us," Georgette mumbled.

Jeffrey found the unexpected remark somewhat unusual but passed it off as casual small talk.

In a few weeks, nevertheless, their commitment to each other would be tested.

Georgette hung around with Jeffrey until the end of his workday. When Jeffrey got a chance, he introduced his wife to Velma. "Georgette, I would like you to meet Velma Dixon. Velma is my front desk operator and office manager."

"Hi Velma, I understand you worked for Jeffrey in Chicago too at the automobile dealership in which he was a partner."

"You're right. I can see he doesn't keep any secrets. Trust and honesty is the only way to go."

"Velma, you are funny. I can see why Jeffrey hired you. You have quite a sense of humor."

"And I can see why he chose you as his wife. We have so much in common."

"Georgette and I will be leaving shortly."

"I'm going to stick around a little longer. I need to return some phone calls."

"I hate to leave you here alone." Jeffrey was concerned for her safety.

"I will be fine. Do not worry about me. I'll make sure the premises are secure before I leave."

"Take care," Georgette said in closing. "I'm glad we finally met."

## Chapter 22

Georgette knelt down at the altar searching for guidance. She had been less than honest with her parishioners and needed their forgiveness. The disheveled part of her life she had hidden was threatening to surface manifesting itself at a time in which she hoped to take her ministry to the next level.

Bowing her head she prayed: Lord let thou will be done. I ask for your understanding and mercy. If I am worthy to lead thou flock in this house, I ask that you bless my effort to do so. If not Lord, I pray that you will let me know thou will."

At the conclusion of her prayer, Georgette walked to her office and booted up her laptop. Attempting to find the right way to address the congregation, she was at a constant lost of words. "I'm going to let the Lord direct me as to what I should say," she stated aloud as tears welled up in her eyes.

"He should always direct our path," Ms. James said as she startled Georgette. "Isn't that right?"

"Yes, you are right," Georgette remarked as she peered towards the door. "I was so wrapped up in my thoughts; I didn't hear you enter."

"What a lovely morning."

"I agree. The Lord has blessed us with yet another day."

"Would you like anything, perhaps some coffee or the morning newspaper?"

"No. I am fine Ms. James."

"If you should think of anything later, don't hesitate to ask. Until a replacement is made for Minister Tucker, it's just the two of us."

True Life Divinity parishioners and others from the community trickled into the over capacity sanctuary. The local news media was on hand for the latest scoop regarding True Life Divinity's deposed pastor. Debra Atkinson was one of many, which stood along the back wall. The deadline Debra had given to Georgette was steadily approaching.

Georgette was ready to bare her soul to the congregation and everyone else that had come. "I would like to come clean," Georgette delivered the shocking opening and waited for the crowd's reaction. A few seconds of random chatter ensued before the building went silent. "Sometimes the record has to be set straight. It is never acceptable to lie under any circumstances," she spoke boldly. "When I applied to become your assistance pastor there was information about my past, which I did not divulge during the selection process. I am asking for your forgiveness. My last semester at seminary, I was impregnated by Minister Thomas Miles of Blessed Truth Baptist Church of Jersey City. Instead of carrying the baby to term, I opted to have an abortion. I should have pursued other options. Again, I am asking for your understanding; I hope you can find it in your heart to forgive me. I have asked the Lord to forgive me. He is always willing to give second chances. If I wasn't just thinking of myself, I could have given the baby up for adoption. If I wasn't just thinking of myself, I could have kept the child and I would have been a good mother. I am willing to step down as your assistant minister; on the other hand, I am willing to compete to be the senior minister to lead this great congregation." Opening her Bible, Georgette turned to where she would take her text. "I would like to transition into my sermon for today. Hopefully, everyone will stay for the Lord's message." She asked everyone to stand for the reading of the Word. Ezekiel 37:3 KJV - 3 And he said unto me, Son of man, can these bones live? And I answered, O Lord God, thou knowest.

Members within the congregation finally were energized as the sermon progressed.

Following the benediction, Georgette went back to her office. Media representatives randomly selected individuals leaving the sanctuary to gauge their reaction to the ouster of Minister Tucker and to Georgette's shocking confession.

Marjorie joined Georgette in her office.

"So you are here to uplift me."

"That's what family is supposed to do. We have to stick together."

"Jeffrey needs uplifting," Georgette countered. "Not me."

"Did he know?" Marjorie asked.

"No. He did not. He found out today along with everyone else in Central Florida."

"How could you have kept a secret like that from someone who without a doubt loves you?"

"I don't expect you to understand," Georgette glumly replied.

"You had an abortion. He deserved to know."

"I did not want to run the risk of him not accepting me as a broken vessel."

"Are you listening to yourself?"

"It should not matter. I terminated my pregnancy from Minister Thomas Miles before I met Jeffrey; granted it was only a few months earlier."

"You made up his mind for him. That wasn't the right thing to do."

"He knows that I love him."

"That being said, you should go home. Jeffrey needs an explanation."

"You are right. I only hope he is there."


An hour later Georgette arrived home. "I understand that you are angry and you probably do not want to hear anything I have to say," Georgette said. "However, I owe you an apology."

"To say I feel anger is an understatement," Jeffrey responded. "You should have told me about your intentions this morning. I could have been spared being humiliated."

"I'm sorry, Darling. I wanted to tell you."

"You withheld information about your abortion for the same reason."

"I love you. If I had told you, we would not be married."

"So tell me about the young minister."

"When I was studying at seminary, I attended a lecture on campus conducted by Minister Thomas Miles of Blessed Truth Baptist Church of Jersey City. Afterwards, Thomas asked me to accompany him to a nearby restaurant. After having dinner, we went to his hotel room. The stay at a luxury hotel with golf and spa was a gift from his congregation for their single pastor at that time given out during their church's anniversary. We got caught up in the flesh and we sinned. I could not handle the thought of having a child conceived out of wedlock."

"So to reiterate; you withheld information because you could not run the risk of losing me."

"I convinced myself it wasn't such a bad thing to do."

"Well you were wrong."

"Please do not turn your back on me. I can handle rejection, but not from my husband. We have always stuck together through good and bad times."

"I'm hurt," Jeffrey muttered.

"And so am I," she countered.

"You want me to show you empathy for which you do not deserve."

"We should try to put this behind us." Georgette pleaded.

"Wounds are not healed overnight," Jeffrey further stated. "To put it simply, you should have told me before informing the rest of the free world."

"I understand, Jeffrey. You don't have to keep reminding me."

"I'm sorry. But you must know how I feel."

"We both need to heal." Georgette's plea for understanding fell on deaf ears.

"That may take some time. You can not flip a switch to make everything alright."

"Today has been very demanding and distressing. We should go to bed."

"I cannot sleep right now. My head is still spinning. You want me to act as if nothing happened. You go ahead. See you in the morning.

## Chapter 23

Georgette went back to her office after presiding over midweek bible study. She received a text. The message simply said: This is Thomas Miles; please give me a call.

She dialed his cell phone. "Thomas speaking."

"Hi Thomas, How are you?"

"I'm fine. How did everything go?" Thomas quizzed.

"I took your advice. I stood before the congregation and leveled with them about our sexual encounter, which lead to my unplanned pregnancy and abortion."

"You did the right thing," Thomas responded.

"How is the first lady of your flock Mrs. Miles faring?" Georgette probed.

"We are no longer together; she is staying with her parents. The bank finished foreclosing on our house."

"I'm sorry. You must be devastated. Whatever happened to people being there for one another through thick or thin?"

"Up until now we have had each other's back."

"So what happened?" Georgette asked.

"I blame myself," Thomas replied. "I should have been a better provider. We were way over our heads in debt; even with my extra income from my speaking engagements."

"One can only imagine the reaction of your congregation once they hear of my confession."

"My church will have to accept me for who I am; if I am to remain their minister.

"That is spoken like a man of great faith."

"Blessed Truth and I have been through a lot over the years."

"I know, life has its hills and valleys," Georgette offered a word of comfort."

"Tithing is way down. Tomorrow we will refinance our church for a second time in four years."

"A church scandal coupled with the mother of the church walking out on you, does not bode well for a church struggling to regain footing."

Look to the Word for the answer. Thomas put forth scripture. Proverbs 3:5,6 KJV - 5Trust in the Lord with all thine heart, and lean not unto thine own understanding. 6 In all thy ways acknowledge him, and he shall direct thy paths.

"And I should recite these Words of wisdom as well," Georgette added. James 5:16 KJV - 16 Confess your faults one to another, and pray one for another, that ye may be healed. The effectual fervent prayer of a righteous man availeth much."

## Chapter 24

Deacon Brandon Roberts and his son Tracy rang the Bradbury's mansion doorbell. Jeffrey promptly answered and greeted his guest. "Come in gentlemen. I am still waiting for the others to arrive. A few other guys, your brother Seth and Antonio the young man I am mentoring should be joining us for our game of pick up basketball. Antonio borrowed his mother's car. He phoned me a few minutes ago saying he was having difficulty finding the house."

"In the meantime, Tracy, and I would like to see your elaborate indoor basketball court that you have been bragging about."

"Right this way."

Deacon Seth Roberts was next to pull into the red brick circular driveway followed by Antonio and the other guys a few minutes later.

Georgette showed them to the rear of the house where Jeffrey, Brandon, and Tracy were taking warm up shots.

Jeffrey and Antonio picked a team to square off against a team with Brandon and Tracy.

The hard fought physical game was exactly what Antonio and Tracy needed. Antonio drove to the hoop throwing down a two-handed 360-degree turnaround dunk as the game ended.

"We are going to need that kind of tenacity if our Black Bears are going to be state champs in our division," Tracy stated.

"Should I take that to mean you are going to try out for the team?" Antonio eagerly sought an answer. "I can be a dominate force in the frontcourt that's if I can get some real help in the backcourt."

"Absolutely my friend, I would love to be a part of a dynamic duo! I am definitely going to try out!"

"Alright man, let's shake on it." Antonio and Tracy performed the latest teen handshake."

Jeffrey looked on marveling in the newly formed friendship. He started out trying to help one young man but he may have helped two in the process.

## Chapter 25

The Minister Advisory Selection Committee met to evaluate applicants to fill Minister's Tuckers vacant position. Georgette had wasted no time in officially submitting her name for consideration. During the meeting, some of those impaneled argued the embattled assistant minister should have been excluded from the process.

"We should be looking for another assistant minister instead of considering her as a candidate to be our next minister." Deacon Brandon Robert's wife, Melinda voiced her disapproval. "She lied to get the position of Assistant Minister, what's to say she is still not hiding something."

"I agree," Sister Bassett said. "True Life Divinity was given the opportunity to oust Minister Tucker for his infidelity and members should be afforded the same opportunity to oust Mrs. Bradbury in lieu of her lying about her character."

"We are going to honor the wishes of the Deacon Board," Chairman Darlene Ricks made it clear the matter was not up for debate. "I'm in charge of seeing that we select qualified candidates. I intend to make sure we keep our focus on our assignment.

# Eddie Johnson

Are we on one accord?" Silence fell over the room. "Let us proceed." From that date forward throughout the remainder of their charge, cooler heads prevailed.

Georgette was accepted as a finalist, prior to the meeting adjourning.

## Chapter 26

Georgette and Ms. James met for lunch at a nearby Caribbean deli. The quaint restaurant was a favored gathering place for members on Sunday mornings between church services.

Marjorie pulled into the parking lot, exited her vehicle, and hurriedly caught up with them as they entered. Georgette greeted and acknowledged her half sister.

"Your timing is perfect," Ms. James said.

"I was going to grab something to eat on the go." Marjorie voiced her initial intention.

"Since we are here you are going to join us," Georgette insisted."

The women placed and received their orders prior to taking a seat at the first available booth.

Ms. James struck up a conversation about the future of the church. "One of the first items on the agenda for True Life Divinity's new pastor will be to oversee the burning of the mortgage on the property, which would put into motion the building phase of our new sanctuary."

"Can you imagine us moving into an edifice full of the latest glitz and glamour with top of the line technology?" Marjorie said with a sense of excitement."

"Sometimes people can get so wrapped up in the physical beauty and attributes of the building that the real reason for joining the church is lost," Georgette spoke with authority.

"Hopefully, you will still be around when the ground is broken," Ms. James noted as she turned to look at Georgette.

"My brother in law has invested heavily in this church," Marjorie responded. "

"That's a mute point," Georgette spoke defensibly. "I have put the matter in the Lord's hand. When the dust settles; I will remain at True Life Divinity either in my current position or as the new minister."

"I can't believe we are having this discussion," Marjorie asserted. I agree with Georgette. "The Lord has forgiven her. She has more than proven herself as a leader."

"Jeffrey needs to become more involved in the church," Marjorie remarked. "Don't you agree, Ms. James?"

"Well the Bible does speak about works. It's only fitting that he should be more involved since his wife serves as our assistant minister."

"What do you have to say for your husband's lack of participation in the church?" Marjorie sarcastically inquired. "He should do more than donate money and tithes."

"The two of you shouldn't past judgment on my man without the facts." Georgette took offense to their comments.

"And what are the facts Mrs. Bradbury?" Ms. James pompously asked.

"Jeffrey is a mentor in our Men's Ministry program, which helps young men in the congregation and within the community to excel spiritually and academically. He volunteered to help a young man shore up his grades to meet the academics requirements that would allow him again to participate on his school's basketball team. Antonio's presence on the court would boost the school chances for a state championship."

"Who is the young man?" Ms. James was curious.

"What about his right to privacy? Should we be even discussing his plight?" Marjorie tried to make a point but it was ignored.

"His name is Antonio Richards." Georgette would disclose.

"Isn't he Tonya Richards' son," Ms. James inquired"

"Yes," Georgette simply replied.

"I know his mother well," Ms. James acknowledged. "Tonya as she is known looks like a model right out of a fashion magazine."

"So the woman is fine, Marjorie said emphatically. "What does that have to do with anything?

"You are insinuating that she will try to get Jeffrey's attention. I know my husband. Jeffrey is only interested in helping her son."

"Georgette, you probably never met Tonya," Ms. James said doubtingly.

"I met her the other week when she brought her son over to Jeffrey's place of work for a fishing outing. She is quite a flirt."

"I agree." Ms. James tried to hammer home her point. "That is why she should not be trusted."

## *Temptation in the Pulpit*

After leaving the restaurant, Georgette quickly bade the ladies well as she rushed back to the church to conduct her second service.

## Chapter 27

Antonio was welcomed back as a returning star on his school's basketball team after raising his grades.

Tonya tuned into a late night sports television special, which focused on the state's high school basketball conferences. She watched intensely as Coach Patrick Bolton was interviewed while his team worked out.

"Are their any stand out players to look out for this year on the Black Bear's roster." The investigative field reporter inquired.

"We are delighted to have senior classman Antonio Richards returning on our updated squad." Coach Bolton spoke as he pointed towards his star. "Antonio showed exceptional ball handling agility near the end of last season when he was inserted into the rotation as our starting point guard."

Tonya smiled as the camera cut to her son.

"How will the chemistry of this team differ from that of last season?"

"We now have a low post player capable of dominating the interior and setting up guys on the perimeter. His name is Tracy Roberts. He made his presence known by his performance during try-outs."

"Enlighten our viewers about Tracy Roberts."

"Tracy is the son of Brandon Roberts who was once a Georgia college basketball standout, which had hopes of turning pro. Brandon's dream was cut short by unfortunate circumstances and he never made the transition."

"I'm sure we will be hearing more about Tracy Roberts and his father going forth. Coach Patrick Bolton thanks for taking the time out of your busy schedule to answer our questions."

"It has been my pleasure."

"You can only be described as an impassioned coach capable of understanding and motivating his team."

Satisfied and still outwardly brimming from watching her son on the sports special Tonya silenced her television and retired to bed.

## Chapter 28

Jeffrey attended midweek Bible study taught by his
lovely wife Georgette. Her weekly lessons focused
on dealing with life problems utilizing biblical solu-
tions. On their way home, Jeffrey steered their new
Mercedes Benz through an electrical thunderstorm
in which countless streaks of lighting cascaded
across the night sky. Another storm of sorts
brewed within the automobile. Georgette should
have taken some of her own advice. Jeffrey started
an innocent conversation but it quickly change to a
discussion of trust.

"Would you like to accompany me to Antonio's
first home game of the season? It will take place
over in Tampa. The team in Tampa has been the
state champs for the last two years."

"I'm glad you are successful with your mentoring. Let's talk about Tonya. Some of True Life Divinity's women, whom I am not going to name,
suggest I keep an eye on Antonio's mother. According to them, Tonya does more than look; she's
more hands on when it comes to married men."

"You aught to check yourself before you start
questioning my integrity. And do you really think I

would allow myself to become obsessed with another woman to the point that I would let her interfere with our marriage."

"So you are admitting that something is going on."

"Woman please, nothing is happening between Tonya and me! That is not to say, I do not have to fend off the opposite sex from time to time."

"This is not funny Jeffrey. You should not be making remarks about being obsessed with another woman."

"I see you were paying attention. I missed spoke by choosing the wrong words to express what I was feeling."

"I've seen the flirtatious witch in action!"

"What did you say? Besides her persona, she is really a nice person.

"I can't understand. Why do you feel the need to defend her?"

"I said there is nothing going on. Granted there are a number of women who would like to be in your shoes and rightfully so. The vast majority only see me for the money and not for who I am."

# Eddie Johnson

Georgette threw her hands up displaying utter disgust as Jeffrey pulled the car into the driveway. "That's it! I don't want to hear anything else!"

## Chapter 29

The list of candidates for the minister of True Life Divinity continued to grow as the deadline to apply drew near. Georgette became weary of her chances once she got whim of some of the big names rumored to be in the hunt. Minister Aubrey Young the assistant pastor for Heavenly Grace Baptist, one of the largest Baptist churches in New York City, stood out as the most formidable threat to her having a successful bid.

Georgette would verify his interest in the position through Ms. James.

"You're here early," Georgette said as she searched for the right words to pry.

"I am a little early. What can I help you with today?"

"Are you familiar with the name Minister Aubrey Young?"

"Why would you ask?" Ms. James queried.

"I hear he is in the running?"

"A letter came across my desk with his name on it. I believe it was addressed to the Minister Advisory Selection Committee. Besides that I have no knowledge of him."

"That being said Ms. James; I should give you a run down on Minister Aubrey Young. He is amongst the most influential young assistant ministers on the east coast. He probably has been waiting for an opportunity to head a mega church like True Life Divinity."

"Okay, I get it. You are worried about your chances if he is in contention. You should not count yourself out. You have a strong following of members. That's perhaps the reason you are still here. The congregation on the other hand does not know Minister Young personally. You may have the upper hand."

Georgette proceeded to her office. She would receive a visit from Deacon Brandon Roberts. "Come on in deacon. You probably have some news to share. Have a seat."

He promptly sat. "How are you, Minister Bradbury?"

"I'm fine, considering all we have been going through." Georgette responded still not sure of the reason for the Deacon's visit.

"I should get to the reason I'm here."

"Hopefully you have some refreshing good news."

"Minister Tucker has refused all offers our attorney has put forth to settle out of court. Sunday morning, I am going to fill the church in with the latest information from our legal council."

"I was hoping he would settle," Georgette replied with a sound of frustration in her voice. "The church needs to heal."

"I agree," Brandon said. "His lawyer's are requesting more than four times the amount we are willing to entertain."

"I don't know what to say. That is unbelievable. We should leave the matter up to the Lord."

Georgette unexpectedly changed topic. "What has Minister Tucker been doing since his ouster?" She asked.

"He is running revivals," Brandon answered. "Turnout has been dismal at times to good. A few of our flock have been seen at his gatherings around town."

"The Lord is always willing to forgive. He may yet be given another chance." Georgette remarked.

"How is Jeffrey handling all the controversy surrounding your past?"

# Eddie Johnson

"I'm surprised that you of all people would ask. My husband and I have always tried to keep our personal life to ourselves. I am blessed to have an understanding husband."

"Minister Bradbury, it's been nice chatting. Take care. I'm going to see myself out."

## Chapter 30

Antonio boarded a bus with the rest of his team-
mates en route to Tampa to take on their intra
state Florida Yellow Jackets high school basketball
rival in their first game of the season. Midway
through the ninety minutes ride on Interstate Highway 4 Antonio received a text from his mother that
she would be at the game. He promptly returned
the message acknowledging its receipt and simply
said thanks. Tonya had gotten permission from her
boss to leave work early to show support for her
son considering all he had recently gone through.
This was a special occasion for Tonya. Jeffrey had
done his part to make sure that her son would be
ready for the season opener.

Even the best plans sometimes go awry. Driving
aggressively along Maitland Boulevard, Tonya cut
off a driver of a sports utility vehicle as she tried to
avoid stopping at yet another traffic light. The busy
eastbound lanes of the thoroughfare grinded to a
halt as the accident blocked traffic. Miraculously no
one was injured. Her car was towed after being
rendered inoperable. Tonya was ticketed for the

accident. She would be given a ride home by the investigating highway patrol trouper.

Tonya's face was drenched with water from a constant flood of tears. The thought of her not being perched in the bleachers pulling for her boy was heart wrenching.

Jeffrey's cell phone rang as he locked his house to head out. "Hello Jeffrey speaking."

"Hi Jeff, I am glad to hear your consoling voice."

"You sound down. Are you okay?"

"I crashed my car on the way home. I am a little shaken."

"Where are you?"

"The highway patrolman working the accident scene gave me a lift home. Antonio expects me to be at his game tonight."

"And you still can be with a little help from me. I am about to hit the road. If you promise to be ready; I will pick you up in about thirty minutes."

"I'll be ready. All you have to do is get here. Thank you. Bye."

Just as she had assured Jeffrey, she was ready. Dressed in a pair of shorts draped in a Jersey sporting Antonio's number, she was waiting out-side in front of her dwelling.

"Shall we go?" Jeffrey said. "If we leave now we should make the tip off."

"I'm ready, if you are. Sometimes I can be such a pain in the derriere."

"Don't be so hard on yourself. Your son expects both of us to be there."

Deacon Brandon Roberts and his wife Melinda noticed Jeffrey and Tonya walking into the gymna-sium making their way to the stands. The two sat together seemingly enjoying each other.

"I wonder if Tonya and Jeffrey rode over from Orlando together." Brandon asked.

"And if so, I would like to know if his wife knows," Melinda added. "I tried to warn Georgette that she could not be trusted. Tonya recently broke off a short-term relationship with another married man. I think he got wind of Jeffrey frequenting her apartment. He did not believe Tonya when she said that Jeffrey was coming over to see her son."

Jeffrey could tell that Tonya was really into the game as she cheered. She was so excited at one point that she swung her arms wide open with one of them hitting Jeffrey squarely in the face. Embarrassed by the incident, Tonya put an arm around his shoulder, looking him closely in the face to see if he was all right, as someone with a camera snapped a picture.

"Go ahead. Root for your boy," Jeffrey replied. He made light of the inadvertent slap in the face. "I'm fine."

The Black Bears would trounce the Yellow Jackets. It was the perfect way to kick off the season by defeating last year's division state champions.

On the way home, Tonya would fall asleep. She would not awaken until Jeffrey was parallel parking his car. After exciting his vehicle, she could not resist the urge; playfully she turned around, smiled, and waved to him as she climbed the stairs on the way to her apartment.

Jeffrey pulled his vehicle into the garage as the digital clock on the dashboard displayed 12:00 am. He would be surprised to see Georgette still waiting up for him. "I thought you would be asleep."

"I would have been but I was glued to the tube watching a Denzel Washington flick," she stated as the movie credits began to roll.

"How was the basketball game?"

"It was great. I only wish you could have gone."

"The Lord's work comes first. I'm sorry you had to go alone."

"I wasn't alone. I gave Tonya Richards a ride over to Tampa to see her boy play."

"What did you say? You did what!"

"Tonya had an accident with her car and I made sure she did not miss her son's season opener. After all, Antonio was depending on her to be in the stands. I thought it was the right thing to do."

"You were hanging out with Tonya. I hope none of my church members were there."

"I'm sorry baby. This is not how I thought you would respond to me helping Tonya."

"You were supposed to help her son. You were not to get personally involved with Tonya.

"Georgette, listen to me; you are the only woman in my life. I would never let another woman come between us."

"I am going to bed. Do not bother to join me! You can sleep on the sofa tonight!"

## Chapter 31

As Georgette walked through the sanctuary's parking lot following a Women's Ministry meeting, she experienced a feeling of being watched.

"Wait up Minister Bradbury. I would like to have a word with you," she heard a low even keeled voice call out.

She turned around as Debra was exiting her vehicle. "Why won't she leave me alone?" Georgette mumbled to her self. "She isn't going to get any money." She kept speaking under her breath as her ex friend approached.

"How are you?" Debra asked.

"I'm fine! What do you want! I'm trying to leave!" Georgette lashed out.

"Give me a few minutes. Hear me out."

"I'm listening, what do you have to say?" Georgette lowered her voice.

"First of all I would like to apologize for trying to extort money from you. I was wrong. Please, forgive me, if you can find it in your heart."

"I have forgiven you."

"I would like to share a bit of information. I have confessed my sins and have rededicated my life to

God. I'm now a member of Ravens Avenue Baptist Church."

"I'm glad you turned your life around."

"Maybe one day I'll finish seminary. I admire the way you handle adversity. Your tenacity and grit has inspired me to be stronger. If I hadn't been so mean to you, I probably would have joined True Life Divinity."

"I am sure Minister Lawton will take good care of you at Ravens Avenue Baptist."

"Do you know him personally?"

"I met him a few times. We are members of the same Baptist Association."

"I was in church the morning you bared your past indiscretions."

"You were standing in the back," Georgette sounded puzzled. "Why did you bother to show?"

"That's a good question. I wish you would have known my intention before you got up to speak. My plan was to tell you once service ended that I would not be following through with my demand."

"I was living a lie by not being upfront with those in my spiritual charge." Georgette acknowledged.

"It's only by the grace of God that you were not removed from your position. Hopefully you will get the promotion you seek."

"It was nice to speak with the old Debra again. I really should be on my way."

"Continue to pray for me. My life is getting better.

"I will," Georgette replied."

"And before I let you go, I would like for you know that my finances are improving. I have a new job. It pays a decent salary with added benefits."

"God is already blessing you. His Word rings true. Romans 8:31 KJV - 31What shall we then say to these things? If God be for us, who can be against us?"

Debra quoted a scripture describing the rededication of her life. Mathew 6:33 KJV - 33 But seek ye first the kingdom of God, and his righteousness, and all these things shall be added unto you.
"Don't be a stranger to True Life. You are always welcome."

## Chapter 32

Jeffrey invited Dexter Jones out to dinner in hopes of making him a minority investor in his company. Georgette had taken time out of her busy schedule to accompany him.

"I have been checking you out online," Dexter noted. The customer reviews for Jeff's Deep Sea Fishing have been mostly great. The media reports on your company have all been positive."

"I should take that to mean you are interested in being a partner. You were high on my list to come aboard even before its inception." Jeffrey reached over and laid his hand upon that of his wife.

"I was thoroughly impressed," Dexter continued with his praise for Jeffrey. "From my point of view, your first day was a complete success."

"Thank you. Gearing up for business involved extensive preparation by everyone on my staff. I credit my office manger Velma Dixon for making the task easy."

"Your husband is quite a man." Dexter said including Georgette in the conversation.

"Yes, that he is," Georgette simply replied. "Jeffrey mentors a young man through an outreach program undertaken by the church's Men's Ministry."

"That's a perfect example of how he impacts lives in a positive way."

"That's my Jeffrey," Georgette again agreed.

They all laughed.

"You two compliment each other well," Dexter commented.

"It's not often two 'A' personalities can coexist in a relationship," Jeffrey responded.

"You are right. They are usually at each other's throat because they are too much alike," Georgette added as she looked over at Jeffrey. "We are more like low key 'A' personalities so our likeness works to our advantage."

"Your company is positioned to steadily improve its bottom line." Dexter's interest was obvious. "According to my legal advisor, you are a seasoned business professional."

Light chatter went forth throughout their meal until Dexter signed on as a minority partner.

## Chapter 33

Assistant Minister Aubrey Young of Heavenly
Grace Baptist stepped out of a chauffeured driven
Limousine as its automatic doors flung open. Followed by his entourage the flashy assistant minister
entered the sanctuary, stopping along the way,
shaking hands, and greeting members as he slowly
made his way towards the pulpit. Georgette saw
him approaching and broke off her conversation
with the church treasurer. "Excuse me, Deacon
Watkins; looks like our guest minister has arrived."
Immediately walking over to greet him, she took
notice of his designer clothing, footwear, and ex-
pensive jewelry. "Minister Young, True Life Divinity welcomes you. We are elated that you of all ministers with a spotless reputation have decided to
grace us with his presence."

"It's an honor to be here," Minister Young replied while planting a kiss on Georgette's outstretched hand. I hope the congregation will not be
taken aback by my grand entrance. My intent is to
win them over. You're more beautiful than I could
have ever imagined."

"I guess you didn't see the ring on my finger."

"Minister Bradbury, I'm aware of you being married. Your husband is a lucky man. In case you wondering there is a Mrs. Aubrey Young."

"Follow me," Georgette instructed the young minister. We should be taking our seats in the pulpit."

After a soul stirring praise team presentation, Georgette introduced the long awaited Minister. "Giving honor first to God, members of the pulpit, our congregation, and guest without any further adieu, I would like to introduce the morning minister. Straight from the Big Apple the next voice you will hear, after the choir sings, will be Aubrey Young the Assistant Minister of Heavenly Grace Baptist Church. Minister Young was applauded as Georgette returned to her seat.

The True Life Mass Choir adorned in heavenly inspired graphic designer robes stood to their feet completely occupying the elevated choir loft. Melinda being backed by the choir sang a solo about standing up to the pressures of the world. True Life's Orchestra sprung to life belting out a familiar tune. Members of the dance troop rushed down the isles to the front of the packed house. The highly spirited dancers would present a well choreographed emotional charged colorful performance in tandem with the musical presentation.

Minister Young took his turn addressing everyone respectfully after giving honor to God. From the book of Matthew, he taught on being humble. Matthew 18: 2,3 KJV - 2 And Jesus called a little child unto him, and set him in the midst of them, 3 And said, Verily I say unto you, Except ye be converted, and become as little children, ye shall not enter into the kingdom of heaven.

At the end of his sermon, Minister Young would wow those in attendance by singing two songs, which followed closely his message.

Standing at an exit after service, Minister Young further acknowledged parishioners.

## Chapter 34

Georgette and Jeffrey found themselves in another intense discussion. His affiliation with Antonio's mother Tonya had now risen to a new level of frustration tearing at their already battered relationship.

"Just when I thought my personal life was back on track; I now have to deal with public scrutiny of our marriage," Georgette was flabbergasted. "I am sick of you! And I'm sick of everything!"

"What is wrong with you?" Jeffrey clearly dumbfounded asked. "I've never seen you this angry before,"

"I had to set Deacon Brandon Robert's wife Melinda straight today. According to her, you are having an affair with Tonya."

"I am confused. What could have caused her to come to that conclusion?"

"Melinda and her husband were at the basketball game when they observed you and Tonya together. Our beloved deacon and his lovely wife sensed adultery being committed."

"You said you set her straight. Why are you still upset?"

"But that wasn't the end of it. My frustration reached a new boiling point this afternoon. I got a call from Marjorie alerting me to a picture of you and Tonya that has gone viral on the internet."

"I don't understand."

"It shows you and your mistress kissing in a photo. It was snapped at the game."

"Tonya is not my mistress. Allow me to explain."

"There is nothing to explain. I went online and checked it out."

"An accurate explanation of the photo would be as follow: Tonya inadvertently hit me in the face while cheering for her son. She put an arm around me and looked me closely in the face to see if I was okay. The angle of the photo undoubtedly made it seem as if we were kissing."

"You are lying."

"I have no reason to lie."

"Jeffrey, you were caught red handed," Georgette growled. "You probably are lying about the accident too."

"It is a public record. You can check the State Highway Patrol's accident website."

"Your work with Antonio is done!" I am forbidding you from any further contact with that loose woman and her boy."

"I promised Antonio that I would be around for him. He expects me to continue going to his games for the remainder of the season."

"I'm trying to be the new minister at True Life Divinity; however, this brewing scandal does not bode well."

"Why not explain the truth to your congregation?"

"You can't be serious."

"Nip this in the bud, before it gets out of hand."

"I'm through arguing." She grabbed her purse.

"And where do you think you are going?" Jeffrey barked.

"Get out of my way, Jeffrey!" Georgette shoved him aside, bolted out of the door, and then slammed it shut.

# Chapter 35

During Men's Ministry meeting, Jeffrey stood before his fellow members to report on the success of his mentorship. A question and answer session ensued before he left the podium. "What was the biggest obstacle that you encountered?" Deacon Perkins asked.

"That's a good question. The biggest challenge I incurred was when I first met Antonio in getting him to open up for communication. His father was a military sergeant, which had recently been killed fighting in Afghanistan."

"How difficult was it to tutor him," Deacon Watkins put forth the next question. "It's my understanding his grades were poor."

"Antonio was just not applying himself to his studies. Academically he was fine until the start of the current school year."

Chairman Brandon Roberts would ask the last question. Jeffrey thought to himself, I hope he doesn't bring up Antonio's mother, Tonya.

"How would you describe the relationship you have forged with Antonio?" Brandon asked.

Jeffrey let out a sigh of relief before responding. "Antonio knows I am there for him as an adult male figure. He knows he can confide in me with life questions. Antonio and I have a lot in common."

While Jeffrey was making his way back to his seat, Chairman Roberts made a suggestion for the others to consider. "I offer a motion that we patronize Jeffrey Bradbury's deep sea fishing operation."

"It's a wonderful idea. I can't wait for us to show our brotherly camaraderie out on the water." Deacon Johnson delighted in the idea.

The motion was accepted, approved, and put on their agenda for the coming year.

## Chapter 36

Tonya drove slowly through the Bangor's Island Community admiring upscale homes and mansions spread out over large acreage lots bearing well-manicured green lawns.

Winding down the beautiful landscaped streets, Tonya fantasized about changing roles with Georgette and having a husband like Jeffrey. She kept daydreaming until she reached her intended destination.

After climbing several steps, she was standing at the French doors of the Bradbury's mansion. Tonya's finger froze on the doorbell. A series of thoughts rapidly crossed her mind as she stood immobilize. I should leave. Suppose I am not welcome. I'm probably going to make a fool of myself.

"May I help you?" Tim the gardener queried.

"I was thinking about visiting Mrs. Bradbury. I'm Tonya Richards."

"You have to press the doorbell, if you expect to enter," Tim teased.

She finally pressed the doorbell sending a beautiful melodic sound throughout the dwelling.

"May I help you," Georgette said as she opened the door.

"I'm Tonya Richards."

"I know who you are. Who are you here to see? Are you here to see Jeffrey? He is not home."

"I'm actually here to see his wife and my assistant pastor, Georgette Bradbury."

"Okay. I am Mrs. Bradbury. You already know me. We met on the opening day of my husband's business. You dropped your son off to go out on its initial fishing outing."

"May I come in for a while?"

"I have things to do. I am listening. What do you want? Make it short."

Tonya entered but decided not to have a seat. "I'm here to address a rumor that I'm having an affair with your husband." Tonya got straight to the point."

"Are you really..."

"Yes," Tonya said emphatically, pausing briefly before resuming. "No matter what you've heard; it's just not true. Nothing is going on between us."

"The picture floating around in cyberspace is quite believable. The internet junkies are having a wonderful time with it. If you were to see it, you would know why.

"I am aware of the photo. The angle of the camera made us appear to be kissing. I'm sorry it has brought shame to your marriage."

"Lord knows I am trying to be humble!" Georgette said hotly. "Jeffrey tried to feed me that same lie!" Georgette words and bodily demeanor suddenly changed to be a little less than holy.

"I've hit a raw nerve with you. Perhaps I should leave."

"No darling. Do not go. What else do you have to say?"

"I tried to plead my case on the church's website blog."

"What happened?"

"I couldn't get it to post."

"That's because it is a family oriented website. The Audio Visual Department screen content to see if it is appropriate."

"Jeffrey probably has already told you everything there is to know about our supposed Tampa fling. You should believe him. Antonio looks up to your husband for guidance. Don't forget my boy also attends True Life Divinity. He is crushed by the things people are saying about his mother."

"Your innocent boy is not the only one affected by my husband's alleged affair with you. I'm trying to be the next minister at True Life. Your connection with my man is not helping my effort."

"I thought you would be more understanding, being a woman of the Lord."

"I have instructed Jeffrey to distance himself from you. Marriage is sacred! And it should not be tampered with!"

"Your husband only gave me a ride to Antonio's game because I wrecked my car. His only concern is for my son. Antonio needs a strong male in his life." Tonya held back tears trying to maintain a strong presence. "You are not going to take that from him."

"Quit pretending to be victimized."

"Minister Bradbury, I beg of you, we should find away to work through this together."

"We shouldn't waste our time. That will never happen." Georgette pointed in the direction of the door. "I think you should go!" She yelled.

"I'll see myself out!" Tonya lashed back. "Some kind of Christian you are." Tonya rushing to leave, mumbled aloud.

Jeffrey arrived home to find Georgette in her private study.

He cracked the door to look in trying not to disturb her concentration.

"Come in honey. How was your day?"

"It was fine. On my way home, I could have sworn Tonya was sitting at the stoplight waiting to exit our prestigious community."

"Your eyes were not deceiving you. Tonya dropped in to redeem herself."

"Tonya is a remarkable woman. You probably gave her hell even though it was not warranted."

"I didn't say anything that she should not have anticipated," Georgette said unapologetically. "My womanly intuition tells me she is hot for you. Look me in the eyes. Tell me that she has never come on to you. Her reputation preceded your involvement."

"I am not going to participate in your mindless game," Jeffrey adamantly shot back.

"She would change places with me in a heartbeat," Georgette candidly implied. "You know I am right. Tonya is not to be trusted. I notice you didn't deny her ever making a play for you."

"You are being delusional, Georgette. You should seek spiritual guidance before you start wrecking lives including yours."

Georgette continued expressing her displeasure. "You should not temp me, I just might leave."

"I stood by you when you were clearly wrong," Jeffrey noted. "Now is the time for you to do the same. I am going to level with you. When I first met Tonya, she showed an interest in me. Other women have done the same. But I have never given into any of them."

"I knew it. The witch is after you."

"You should come down off your high pedestal. Admit it. Men have come on to you too. I suspect you did not entertain any of their offers."

"You are the one in the wrong." Georgette said grumpily.

"I was able to forgive Tonya and I was able to move on to help her son. That was the Christian thing to do." Tired of trying to reason with Georgette, Jeffrey quietly left the room.

## Chapter 37

Georgette was waiting at Orlando International Airport for her flight home to visit her parents in Chicago when an unlikely chance meeting with Thomas Miles took place. He was in town for a speaking engagement.

Thomas would spot Georgette prior to her departure. "Where are you going?" He spoke while making his way through a crowd."

"Hi Thomas, I am going home to Chicago for a few days. I did not expect to see you. What brings you to Orlando?"

"I'm here to attend a prosperity workshop by Minister Melvin Peters. He is a local minister; you've probably heard of him."

"When we last talked your church was in the process of refinancing." Georgette said.

"The new mortgage was approved," Thomas eagerly provided an update. "Blessed Truth has a new lease on life."

"Thank God. You had a financial breakthrough."

"Your hunch was correct. "Once you confessed to being impregnated by me and having a subsequent abortion, media ascended on Blessed Truth like vultures. A few select members of my congregation without hesitation called for a special meeting to oust me. I was surprised when the majority of the members voted in my favor. Thank God, I am still in the pulpit."

"And the Lord will continue to bless our ministries as long as we put him first." Georgette said.

"On another note, a sister church locally will be merging with Blessed Truth. We feel by uniting we will be better off financially."

"Both houses of worship will undoubtedly lose parishioners in the transition." Georgette surmised.

"Blessed Truth's membership will still almost double." Thomas provided an upside to the merger. "I would love to see the church involved in more community outreach programs."

Georgette decided to share her own dilemma. "I am currently going through problems in my marriage. Jeffrey may have fallen for a harlot."

"What did you say?"

"Jeffrey may have fallen for a prostitute. He denies it but has yet to convince me otherwise."

"Your marriage is probably salvageable."

"And yours is not…" Georgette paused from speaking and waited for a response.

"I doubt my wife and I will ever reunite."

"I'm sorry, I screwed up your marriage," she sympathized.

"Don't beat yourself up about my marriage. Brenda had already run home to her parents when our finances went sour. I am prepared for the inevitable. I should be served with divorce papers any day now."

"I have a gut feeling something else went wrong between you and Brenda other than your finances."

"Couples should trust and believe in one another. Those are attributes Brenda and I no longer possess."

"My flight has arrived," Georgette stated as she reached for her carry on luggage."

"Have a nice trip," Thomas said. "Keep in touch."

"I'll say a prayer for you," Georgette lifted her voice, glancing over a shoulder, as she rushed off to get in line to board her flight. "We'll talk later via phone when our schedules allows."

## Chapter 38

The phone rang at Tonya's apartment. "Hello, To-nya speaking."

"Hi Tonya, I would like to continue mentoring Antonio; but that might not be possible."

"I understand. Your wife has already made it clear that you are to stay away from me and my son."

"You are right," Jeffrey said. "As a result of her ultimatum, I will no longer be coming over."

"I plan to continue going to his basketball games as I had promised.

"I think you have done enough for him even if you don't attend anymore of his games."

"Let him know my cell phone still works."

"I will let him know. The two of you are overdue for a talk."

"Where is Georgette?" Tonya pried.

"She's away for a few days visiting her mom and pop in Chicago."

"Don't forget to clear my number out of your cell phone call history."

"Georgette would never invade my privacy."

"Don't be so sure. If I were in her shoes, I would snoop."

"And Georgette would not," Jeffrey exclaimed.

"I hope by helping my son, you have not hurt your wife's chances of becoming our next pastor."

"You are not at fault, no matter how the members vote," Jeffrey reassured Tonya.

"I'm going to hang up," Jeffrey said. "Georgette is calling me on my other line. Bye."

"Hello."

"Hi honey. I'm calling to let you know I am in Chicago.

"Hi Georgette, I'm glad you arrived safely. How was the flight?"

"It was okay. We encountered some turbulent weather along the way."

"Apologize to your mom and dad for me not making the trip."

"Alright, I am going to let you go. I know you must have a million things to do."

"Not really. I love you."

"I love you more," she cooed. See you in a few days."

## Chapter 39

On the last day of Georgette's Chicago visit Susan sat at the breakfast table chatting with her daughter. Georgette hoped her mother would provide her with advice on how best to deal with her problems.

"How can I be sure that Jeffrey is not lying when he tells me that he is not having an affair?"

"Sometimes you can tell by a change in a person's speech or bodily mannerisms when questioned," Susan spoke as she tried to think of how best to answer her daughter's question. "For instance, Marjorie's father would scratch out his hair every time he lied to me about not cheating. In my marriage to your father Carlton infidelity has never been an issue."

"I guess Jeffrey would pass your test with flying colors."

"Tell me about the woman which Jeffrey is alleged to be involved."

"Her name is Tonya Richards. Tonya is an extremely beautiful woman. She loves to flirt with married men. Jeffrey admitted she expressed an interest in him but contends nothing happened because he set her straight."

"In other words, Jeffrey let it be known that he doesn't mess around."

Georgette decided she would not bring up the matter of the photo. She already had started feeling better.

"I think you should give Jeffrey the benefit of the doubt unless you have more damaging evidence to back up your belief that he is not being truthful."

"I still may be affected adversely by this unfortunate revelation in my bid to be elevated from my current position."

"You have been good for True Life Divinity as their assistant minister and the members should remember that when it comes time to elect their next senior Minister.

After finishing breakfast and loading the dishwasher, Georgette and her mom headed out for a day of shopping.

## Chapter 40

Georgette having rapped up a few days off in Chicago flew back to Orlando on a Saturday night.

The next morning, Georgette assumed her position in the pulpit. Antonio and his mother were seated front and center of the sanctuary. Tonya waved at Georgette to make her presence known.

The morning announcements were read by Sister James. Before returning to her seat, she introduced Antonio to the congregation. "We will now hear from Antonio Richards. Antonio is one of True Life Divinity's more popular youth."

"Good morning church." A well mannered young man began to speak. "I would like to give special recognition to someone dear to me; his name is Mr. Jeffrey Bradbury. You all know him as our assistant pastor's husband. To make a long story short, my father passed away fighting overseas in the war. Due to the loss of my father, I had given up on school and my plans for the future. If Mr. Bradbury had not stepped in as my mentor, I would have blown my senior year in high school. So if you hear of me as a rising basketball prodigy, aspiring to play professionally, remember to thank him for getting my life back on track." Antonio pointed in the direction of Jeffrey, as he briefly stood to his feet, while receiving a warm round of applause. "I also love my mother Mrs. Tonya Richards. Unfortunately, a misleading photograph has been circulating on the internet. I witnessed firsthand what took place when the picture was snapped. Mr. Bradbury had given my mother a ride to see me play over in Tampa since she had wrecked her car earlier the same day. Again, I will try to abbreviate a long story. I had just sank a three point shot out on the court resulting in our team taking a one point lead, my mother jumped to her feet emotionally celebrating when she inadvertently hit Mr. Bradbury in the face. She placed a hand on his left shoulder as she turned to look him in the face making sure that he was okay. Someone took a photo from a bad angle, which would later be use to smear my mother Tonya's reputation. I beg of you, please don't think badly of my mother. She has always been a respectable woman with a very delightful outgoing personality. Mom and I have placed social media rebuttals in response to the crude allegation.

# Eddie Johnson

Georgette faced her congregation rejuvenated from hearing the young man speak. She gave honor to God and acknowledged everyone in attendance. "Antonio Richards could be a hard act to follow." Georgette joked, triggering laughter. "I would like to say that I am proud of my husband. He never ceases to amaze me when it comes to helping others. There is something to be said about Antonio's mother too. Tonya Richards has to be a great woman to have raised such an intelligent young man. Evilness in the world sometimes tries to destroy that which is meant to be good." Directly eyeing Tonya, she uttered her next remark. "Tonya the Lord loves you; hold your head high." Georgette took her text; and after the youth choir sang, delivered her message as the morning slowly progressed.

The congregation adjourned and Jeffrey followed Georgette to her office.

"I think someone owes me an apology." Jeffrey made light of what had been a serious situation.

"Were you not listening? What I said in front of the church was more than an apology."

"I know. Antonio's statement actually helped as well. Perhaps we will be viewed again as a couple capable of being a first family."

"I certainly hope so. Two weeks remains before we find out who will be the new head minister of this great house."

"I hope nothing else happens to hinder your chances of filling that role."

"I am ready to go dear," Georgette said as she grabbed her briefcase."

## Chapter 41

The long awaited Sunday arrived for True Life's parishioners to select a new advocate of God to head their flock. Sitting in the special afternoon meeting Jeffrey sensed Georgette's nervousness as she murmured what she hoped would not be the inevitable outcome.

Deacon Brandon Roberts after providing a brief history of the church explained the election process as ushers handed out ballots allowing members adequate time to make their selections. Afterwards the forms were collected and put away for safe storage. The votes would be tabulated at the end of the week once the deadline for write in votes passed and the results would be revealed the following Sunday.

The pastor's selection committee met the next night to finalize plans for the pastor's installation. It would take place 30 days from the announcement of the new pastor. Doctor Floyd Mc cay from Deliverance Baptist Church of Atlanta would preside over the auspicious occasion.

## Temptation in the Pulpit

The week flew giving way to the highly anticipated Sunday. Georgette leaned forward in her
seat. Deacon Brandon Roberts composed himself
standing at the podium. He situated the paper with
the election results squarely on the podium in from
of him. "It is an honor to stand before everyone to
announce our next senior minister. Thousands of
votes were cast; however, only a few hundred decided the winner." Deacon Roberts provided the
exact number tallied for each candidate.

Georgette sprung to her feet as True Life Divinity's new senior minister. The spiritual leader
felt as if she had scaled the rough side of a mountain. Members arose to their feet with an arousing
hand of applause. "I would like to thank my heavenly father and you all for seeing past my faults."
She sounded sincere and humble. Tears trickled
down her face. "By the grace of God I am here.
And by God's grace I would like to do his will at
True Life Divinity for many years to come." After a
brief pause, she proceeded to take her text for the
morning, which focused on the goodness of God.

After worship, she was approached by Minister
Aubrey Young who had been conspicuously sitting

in the back of the facility. Minister Young had arrived without the grandiose entrance and pompous fanfare of his last visit. The dispirited minister shook hands with Georgette and provided her with a warm friendly embrace.

"Minister Bradbury, I would like to congratulate you. God's people have spoken."

"Thank you. You ran a good race. The vote was close. The Lord has shown favor to me and for that I am grateful."

"I should let you go."

"It was nice to see you again. Take care, Minister Young.

"I'm looking forward to spending time with my wife and our two kids checking out the local tourist attractions before heading back to the big city."

As he was speaking his wife, Andrea tapped him on the shoulder. "Are you ready to go dear? The children are waiting outside."

"Minister Bradbury this is Andrea my lovely wife."

"Hi Andrea," she spoke extending a hand of welcome.

"Minister Bradbury, I am honored to be in your presence. Good luck as the new minister of True Life Divinity."

"If I stay within the will of the Lord, I should be fine," Georgette replied marveling in Andrea's show of confidence in her ability to lead.

"Hopefully we will meet again," Andrea stated.

"I am extending an invitation for you and your man of God to again worship with us in the future," Georgette replied.

Afterwards, Georgette went straight home still relishing in the outcome of her hard fought battle.
Chapter 42

True Life Divinity's sanctuary bristled with casual chat from the members as they patiently awaited Georgette's installation. Her proud parents flew into town the night before so as not to be late for the ceremony. Carlton and Susan had accompanied their daughter to both Sunday morning services. The guest speaker for the day was Minister Floyd Mc cay of Deliverance Baptist Church. Several members of his congregation had traveled with him from Atlanta. He was now ready to preside over the evening event in which Georgette officially would take over her new role.

Deacon Thaddeus Watkins a senior member of the church set the tone with an opening prayer acknowledging their new leader, and thanking God for sending her their way.

Georgette would be treated to something she never anticipated. As the True Life Divinity Mass Choir stood to their feet the guest soloist made her way to the microphone. Unaware Marjorie was now a member of the choir; Georgette was totally surprised yet delighted to hear her half sister sang. Marjorie performed a song written specifically for the occasion by the choir director Nora Holmes. As she belted out the moderately tempo tune simply titled 'Beholding to His Grace'. Georgette emotionally overwhelmed by the musical selection wiped away tears.

The minister for the evening, Doctor Floyd Mc cay provided a message focused on the responsibilities of the new leader of their house of worship. "The duties of a minister should never be taken lightly. Ministers should always conduct themselves in an appropriate manner according to biblical teachings." The Word of God presented was full of information for the new minister, although not quite the length of a usual sermon.

Minister Mc cay also presented the charge outlining what is expected of the disciple in her new capacity. Georgette response was simply "I will" as she gracefully accepted the responsibilities that come with her elevated role. The congregation followed by accepting the charge to uphold their responsibilities to the church leader, which includes holding their new minister accountable to her commitment.

Minister Mc cay offered a blessing over Georgette. He prayed while laying a hand on her forehead as she knelt and the congregation outstretched their hands in a symbolic lying of their hands as well.

At the conclusion of the ceremony, members of the congregation were treated to dinner in the church dining hall. Georgette briefly met with the parishioners, which gathered offering a blessing over the food. She thanked those who supported her and stressed that she looked forward to working with the entire church.

After leaving the sanctuary, Georgette joined her parents, Jeffrey, Marjorie, and Minister Mc cay for dinner at Zoey's Bahamian Eatery. An invitation was extended by the minister from Atlanta for his newly found friends to visit his church. "Minister Carlton Hatcher of the Heaven's Shore Baptist Church of Chicago, you are a well known respected figure in the Christian world," Minister Mc cay noted. "And should you decide to visit Deliverance Baptist Church of Atlanta it would be an honor to have you deliver a Sunday morning message."

"I would be willing to do a full week of revival," Carlton interjected as he finished his statement.

"Your daughter is also a dynamic speaker. We could have her speak on two of the nights."

"The revival is a great idea," Georgette enthusiastically responded."

On a bright Saturday afternoon, True Life Divinity Baptist Church's mortgage burning and groundbreaking ceremony for their new sanctuary flung into full swing. Georgette stood on the property in the area where the pulpit would grace their new house of worship.

"My fellow members, I have some good news. Earlier today, I found out from our Deacon Board Chairman that Minister Tucker has dropped his civil lawsuit against True Life Divinity." A loud cheer went out from the huge crowd that had gathered.

Everyone attentively looked on as she proceeded with a brief word. "We should give thanks to our Lord and Savior. He has aloud us to arrive at this point to embark on the True Life Divinity Baptist Church's 30ᵗʰ year anniversary." Georgette thought to herself about the surreal moment unfolding in her life. *In less than a year, I have risen from the assistant minister to standing before this great church as their leader in celebrating a milestone in their long history.* Georgette finished her brief talk; a mini concert was provided by the choir, and a few members read bible verses that were fitting for the occasion.

Setting fire to the mortgage in preparation of breaking ground for their new edifice, Georgette reflected on how she overcame her past faults, which were forgiven by God. *The road was short and sometimes bumpy but I kept my unrelenting faith in the Almighty.*

# ABOUT THE AUTHOR

Eddie Johnson is a Florida native that continues to evolve as an author constantly refining his writing. At an early age, he discovered this unique gift. With the urging of his spouse, he decided to share the results of his literary prowess with the world. For now and the foreseeable future he will continue to transform life experiences into interesting storylines. Billionaire's Retreat, a romance, murder mystery, and suspense thriller is one of his most recent works. He also has a poetry book titled Reaching For Celestial Heights. The focus of this African American fiction writer is on urban romance, church drama, murder mystery, suspense, and dramatic street related topics. Throughout his life, he has held jobs assisting others. For over a decade, he worked as a Public Assistance Specialist with the State of Florida. Since then he has worked in private sector customer relations and billing related positions in telecommunications and banking. He has a Degree in Business Data Processing. Eddie is a devoted husband and father.